Fergus Hume

The Man with a Secret

Vol. III

Fergus Hume

The Man with a Secret
Vol. III

ISBN/EAN: 9783337053086

Printed in Europe, USA, Canada, Australia, Japan

Cover: Foto ©Andreas Hilbeck / pixelio.de

More available books at **www.hansebooks.com**

THE MAN WITH A SECRET.

A Novel.

BY

F E R G U S   H U M E,

Author of

"THE MYSTERY OF A HANSOM CAB," "MADAME
MIDAS," "THE PICCADILLY PUZZLE," " MISS
MEPHISTOPHELES," ETC., ETC.

There are those in this world whose egotism is so
profound, that they look upon creation as designed for
their sole benefit, and take advantage of all opportunities
furnished by Fate, to gain unto themselves exceeding
riches and honour, although prosperity to one may mean
ruin to many.

IN THREE VOLUMES.

VOL. III.

LONDON:
F. V. WHITE & CO.,
31, SOUTHAMPTON STREET, STRAND.
1890.

CONTENTS.

TO

My Dear Father,

JAMES HUME,

This Book is Affectionately Dedicated

By His Son,

FERGUS.

The mocking fiend who near us stands
    Entices us to evil deeds ;
He binds our souls in sensual bands
    The mocking fiend who near us stands ;
But some good woman-angel pleads
    For mercy at Almighty hands ;
With such for guide what mortal heeds
    The mocking fiend who near us stands ?

THE MAN WITH A SECRET

CHAPTER I.

THE BITTERNESS OF DEATH.

We call Death harsh, but death ends all our strife,
Dishonour turns to gall the sweetest life.

To say that those who had assembled in
the drawing-room of the Grange to hear
the will read were astonished at the extraordinary disclosures they had heard,
would give but a faint idea of the
amazement they felt. That the squire
should have left his large fortune to a
son of whom no one had ever heard was
most remarkable, but that the son in
question should turn out to be Reginald
Blake was almost beyond belief.

Still, after examining all the evidences

of the fact, Mr. Bolby came to the conclusion that there could be no doubt as to the identity of the young man.

According to the story told by Patience Allerby, who was well known to be the nurse of the boy, he had been born at Chelsea, London, six months after Fanny Blake's arrival there, and had been called by his mother's name. On bringing him down to the village, Randal Garsworth, no doubt dreading the scandal, refused to recognise his son, but agreed to pay for his keep. Patience, therefore, had done the best she could under the circumstances, and had placed the boy with Dr. Larcher, telling him that his parents were dead, thus giving him at least the fiction of an honourable birth. It had been a lie, no doubt, still it was a lie the nobility of which there was no denying, and one which would hardly be set down by the Recording Angel.

As to the strange discovery that had been made, everyone saw at once that the squire had tried to make tardy reparation for his sin by leaving his property to his unfortunate son; and the evidence of the will itself, the evidence of the letter found in the squire's desk, and the evidence of the seal ring, all showed plainly that the young man was really and truly the mysterious son alluded to in the will. Besides, according to Dr. Larcher, the squire had mentioned Reginald's name on his death-bed, and pointed towards the desk, intimating, no doubt, that the document which would give the young man his just right was hidden there, as indeed it was. Altogether, on reviewing the whole case through, Mr. Bolby declared it to be the most extraordinary one that had ever come under his notice. There could be no doubt but that justice had been done, and Reginald was formally recognised by everyone as the master of Garsworth Grange.

Of course, the absence of registration and baptismal certificates would doubtless have proved a stumbling-block in a court of law, but, as Beaumont had foreseen, there was no hesitation upon Una's part to surrender the property to one whom she believed to be the rightful heir, and moreover, when Mr. Bolby discovered that the two claimants were engaged to be married, he declared that it was a very neat solution of the difficulty, although as a matter of fact, owing to the clearness of the case on the one side and the refusal to test its truth by legal process on the other, no such difficulty had ever arisen.

Beaumont was now extremely satisfied with the way in which his conspiracy had succeeded, as he had placed his

son in possession of a fine estate, worth
ten thousand a year. Now his next object was to gain control of this large
income through the young man himself.
Thanks to his ingratiating manner, he
completely succeeded in fascinating
Reginald, who admired him greatly, and
Beaumont only wanted to have the
young man in his company for a few
months to become indispensable to him.
He proposed to become Reginald's right-
hand man, at a fixed salary, and with autho-
rity to look after the estate, out of
which he foresaw he could make some
nice pickings. To do this, however, he
would have to get Reginald away from
the village, as Patience jealously watched
her son, and if she thought for one
moment that Beaumont was trying to
take advantage of his lack of worldly
experience, was quite capable of exposing
the whole swindle.

Fate, however, once more played into his hands, for Mr. Bolby, having recognised Reginald as the heir, insisted upon his coming up to London to see his partner, and be put in formal possession of the estate. Beaumont, therefore determined also to go to London first, so as not to arouse the suspicious nature of Patience Allerby, and then call on Reginald when he arrived later on. Once he had an interview with him in London he was quite satisfied that he could do what he liked with the plastic nature of the young man.

On his part Blake, or, as he was now called, Garsworth, was anxious to leave the village for a time till the nine days' wonder was over, for in spite of the consolatory feeling of having ten thousand a year he felt his position bitterly. Having been brought up in an English gentleman's household, he had imbibed rigorous principles all his life, therefore it seemed to him a terrible disgrace to have such a stigma on his name. He was a nobody—a nameless outcast, unrecognized by the law of England—and much as he wanted to marry Una, he shrank from giving her a name to which he had no legal claim. He dreaded lest there should be children of such a marriage, in which case they would have to bear the stigma attached to their father's birth, and he spoke seriously to Dr. Larcher about releasing Una from her engagement and restoring to her the property to which he felt she was justly entitled. Thus were the fruits of Beaumont's crime placed in jeopardy by the honour and upright feeling of the young man whom such crime had benefited, but luckily for Mr. Beaumont, Una came to the rescue.

She plainly told Reginald that she did

not care for the circumstances of his
birth, which he could not help in any
way, and as to her being rightfully
entitled to the property, if she married
him the property would be just as much
hers as if it had been duly left to her
by the squire. So after a great deal of
persuasion from Una and Dr. Larcher,
Reginald came to accept his somewhat
unpleasant position with equanimity.

"I cannot stay here, however," he
said bitterly. "Everyone stares at me as
if I were a wild beast. I will go up to
town with Mr. Bolby, and return in a
few months, when I get more used to
the position."

Una fully approved of this, and agreed
to stay on at the Grange with Miss
Cassy until he returned, then they
would be married, and go abroad for a
year, during which time the old house
would be redecorated, and they would

then return to live in it, when all the circumstances of his succession to the property had to some extent been forgotten.

Beaumont, having heard this decision, determined to go up to Town in advance and there await Reginald's arrival. So, after taking an effusive farewell of everyone, he departed, carrying with him the good wishes of all with whom he had come in contact. Only Patience did not wish him God speed, but surveyed him grimly when he came to say good-bye to her.

"I'm glad to see you go," she said coldly. "Our son is now provided for, and you have at least done something towards repairing your villainy. I hope I'll never set eyes upon you again, but if ever I hear of you meddling with Reginald in any way it will be the worse for you."

"Say the worse for both of us," retorted Beaumont airily. "We're in the same box over this affair, and punishment to me means the same for you."

So he took his departure, leaving an excellent impression behind him, and every one hoped he would come back again some day, which he laughingly promised to do if his engagements would permit him.

"I'll see you in London, Reginald," he said to the young man, "and anything I can do for you there, of course, you may command me."

Reginald thanked him for his kindness, little thinking how treacherous that kindness was, and then addressed himself to the work of preparing for his own departure.

He had a long interview with Patience, in which she informed him that the story told by her to Dr. Larcher had been told with the best intentions to spare him the truth, and on consideration he saw for himself that she had acted for the best, so he forgave her for the falsehood. Patience stayed on at the Grange, living her old life, and felt quite satisfied now that the future of the human being she loved best on earth was secured.

Reginald asked Dr. Larcher to let him take Dick to Town, which request the worthy vicar granted, only admonishing Mr. Bolby to look carefully after the pair.

"I love them as my own sons," said the good man gravely, "and I dread lest they should be led into evil ways in the great city—they are young and untried—let them not drink, for what says Horace? ' *Non ego sanius, Bacchabor Edonis.*'"

"They won't get any bad example from me," said Mr. Bolby, "from me there's no bad example to be got. I'll take them to the theatres and several amusements, but that's all."

So the vicar, full of anxiety for his dear boys, allowed them to go, and the last to bid Reginald farewell was Una.

"Don't forget me among all the beauties of London," she whispered archly, "or I'll come to Town to look for you."

"Don't be afraid," he replied with an affectation of lightness he was far from feeling. "I will come back to you heart-whole, and then if you'll have me we'll be married."

So the poor lad departed, having learned already thus early in life that wealth alone does not bring happiness.

CHATTER II.

FROM DR. NESTLEY'S POINT OF VIEW.

So low—so low—yes I am low indeed,
But he thy lover, tho' of high estate,
Will fall to this—I tell thee dainty dame
The devil even now is at his ear,
Breathing temptations in most subtle guise,
Which soon will lose him all he holds most dear.

THE autumn was now nearly over, and it was that bleak, chill season just before winter, when the trees, denuded of foliage, seemed to wait for the snow to cover the bare branches, which shivered complainingly in the chill wind. Under foot the ground was dark and sodden, overhead the sky dull and lowering, while piercingly cold blasts blew across the lonely marshes and whistled shrilly over the waste moorland.

Dreary and desolate as it had looked in summer time, Garsworth Grange appeared even more dreary and desolate under the sombre-coloured sky. The damp had discoloured the white marble of the statues, which seemed lost amid the surrounding desert of bare trees and dead leaves. It was everlastingly raining, and Una, looking out of the antique windows at the gloomy landscape seen through the driving mists of rain, felt dull and depressed. All day long the winds whistled through the dismal rooms, and the rain ceaselessly dripped from the eaves, so it was hardly to be wondered that both Una and Miss Cassy felt anything but cheerful.

It was now about two months since Reginald had gone up to Town, and Una had received frequent letters from him about the way in which everything was being arranged by the lawyers. Of late these letters had become feverish in tone, as if the writer were trying to invest his correspondence with a kind of fictitious gaiety he was far from feeling, and this sudden change of style gave her serious uneasiness. She knew how sensitive Reginald was, and how deeply he had felt the discovery of his real birth, so dreaded lest, to banish the spectres which haunted him he should plunge into dissipation. In one of his letters also he had mentioned having met Beaumont in town, and as Una learned from the vicar that Dick Pemberton had gone to Folkestone to see his uncle, she felt doubtful as to the wisdom of an inexperienced youth like Reginald being left alone in London with a reckless man of the world like Beaumont.

She had mistrusted Beaumont when she first met him, but by his fascinating manner he had succeeded in overcoming her repugnance, but now that he was away the influence of his strong personality died

out, and she began to dread his power
over her lover's honourable, guileless
nature.

"I wish Reginald would come back at
once," she said to Miss Cassy, "and then
we could be married, and he would have
some one to look after him.

"I'm sure I'll be glad when you are
married," whimpered Miss Cassy, whose
spirits the lonely life she was leading sadly
depressed. "I'll go melancholy mad if I
stay here—I know I shall. I'm sure that
isn't odd, is it? I feel like what's her-name
in the Moated Grange, you know—the
weary, weary dead thing, I mean, and the
gloomy flats—not half so nice as the flat
we had in town. If we could only go to it
again—I feel so shivery."

And so Miss Cassy rambled on in a
disconnected fashion, one thought suggest-
ing another, while Una sat staring out of
the window, with Reginald's last letter in

her hand, wondering what was best to be done.

"I don't trust Mr. Beaumont," she said at length.   "He is not a good companion for Reginald."

" Oh, my dear," said Miss Cassy, picking up the tea cosy, which she kept by her to put on her head when she felt cold, " such a charming man—quite a Lord what's-his-name in his manners."

"His manners are all right, I've no doubt," returned Una drily, " but what about his morals?"

Miss Cassy gave a little girlish scream, and extinguished herself with the tea-cosy.

" What dreadful things you do say, Una," she observed in a shocked tone.   " So very odd—quite like Zola, so very French.

" My dear aunty, I know you are one of those people who think that unmarried girls should be absolutely ignorant of such things.   I don't agree with you.   There's no need of them to parade their knowledge of evil, but they cannot help hearing about it, however carefully they are brought up. I know London is not a good place for a young man with plenty of money, especially when he is so inexperienced as Reginald— besides, Mr. Beaumont is a man of the world, who I really believe lives by his wits— and if it be a case of his wits against Reginald's, my dear aunt, I'm afraid poor Reginald will come off worst."

"What's to be done, then?" said Miss Cassy blankly. "Do you think if I sent dear Reginald some tracts——"

"I don't think that would be much use," interrupted Una laughing. "No, I'll go over to Garsworth to see the vicar—he will know what is best to be done. I will show him Reginald's letter, and I'm sure he will agree with me that it will be wise to withdraw him from Mr. Beaumont's influence."

"Why doesn't Mr. Bolby look after him?" said Miss Cassy indignantly.

"I daresay Mr. Bolby has got his own business to look after," replied Una with a faint sigh; "besides, he only regards Reginald from a monetary point of view, nothing more — will you come to the vicarage with me, aunt?"

"Oh yes, dear," cried Miss Cassy with great alacrity, "the walk will do me good, and I'm so dull—I'll talk to dear Mrs. Larcher, you know, she's so odd, but still she's better than one's own company, isn't she, dear?—let us get ready at once—the rain has gone off, I see."

"Then let us follow the example of the rain," said Una with a laugh, and the two ladies went away to prepare themselves for their walk.

When they sallied forth with heavy cloaks and thick boots, they found that for once the sun had shown his face and was looking through the watery clouds in a somewhat feeble fashion.

The ground under foot was wet and spongy, still it was better than being immured in the dreary Grange, and as they walked rapidly along their spirits rose in spite of the depressing influence of the weather.

When they arrived at the bridge after a sharp walk they saw a man leaning over the parapet looking at the cold grey water swirling below.

"Dear me, Una, how very odd," exclaimed Miss Cassy, "there is Dr. Nestley."

"Dr. Nestley," echoed Una, rather startled. "I thought he had gone away last week?"

"He was going, but for some reason did not," answered Miss Cassy, who by some mysterious means heard all the gossip of the village. "I hear he is still staying at

Kossiter's—drinking, my dear—oh dreadful
—so very odd."

By this time they were directly in
the centre of the bridge, and hearing
footsteps Nestley turned round, showing
a wan, haggard face, with dull bleared
eyes filled with mute misery. So ill and
desolate did the young man look that Una's
heart smote her as she thought the change
was brought about through her refusal to
marry him, and though she despised him
for his weakness of character in thus being
influenced, yet she still felt pity for the help-
lessness of the poor fellow.

Nestley flushed as he recognized the
two ladies, then raised his hat, and
without saying a word turned once
more to look at the river. Una felt
uneasy as he did so, for a sudden doubt
arose in her heart as to whether he did not
intend to put an end to his life, so taking a
sudden resolution she whispered to Miss

Cassy to walk on by herself to the vicarage.

"I will join you soon," she said in a low voice, "but first I want to speak to Dr. Nestley."

"But it's so odd," objected Miss Cassy, " really so very—very odd."

Nevertheless she made no further objection, and trotted away through the village street, leaving Una alone on the bridge with Dr. Nestley. Though the unhappy young man knew that she was still behind him he did not turn round, but kept staring dully at the foam-streaked waters of the Gar.

"Dr. Nestley," she said, softly touching him on the shoulder, "I want to speak to you."

He turned sullenly round, though the touch of her gloved hand sent a thrill through his frame, and Una recoiled with an exclamation of pity as she saw what a

wreck he was.   His face, formerly so fresh-
coloured, was now grey and thin, his eyes
bleared with dark circles under them, while
his nervous lips and shaking hands showed
how deeply he had been drinking.   Even
in his clothes she saw a change, for they
were carelessly put on ; his linen was dirty
and his tie arranged in a slovenly manner—
altogether he looked like a man who had
entirely lost his self-respect, and cared
neither for his health nor appearance.

Nestley saw the expression on her face
and laughed, a hollow, mirthless laugh,
which seemed quite in keeping with his
wretched appearance.

" You are looking at your work, Miss
Challoner," he said bitterly, " well, I hope
you are satisfied."

Una's pride was up in arms at once.

" You have no right to speak to me in
such a manner, sir," she said haughtily,
looking at him with a proud, cold face.

"Do not ascribe your own folly to any fault of mine—that is both weak and unmanly."

The wretched creature before her drooped his head before the severe gaze of her eyes.

"You would not marry me," he said weakly, "you would not save me from myself."

"Am I to go through the world saving men from their own passions?" she returned scornfully. "Shame upon you, Dr. Nestley, to take refuge behind such a weak defence. Surely because a woman refuses to marry a man he ought not to lower himself as you have done, and then lay the blame on her instead of himself— you ought to make an end of this folly."

"Just what I was thinking," he muttered, glancing at the river. She instinctively guessed what the glance meant, and looked at him, saying :

"Would you add suicide to the rest of your follies?—that is a coward's refuge and one not worthy of a clever man like you. Come, Doctor Nestley," she continued, laying a kind hand on his shoulder, "be advised by me. Give up this mad love of drink which is lowering you to the level of the brutes, and go back to your home — there amid your old companions you will soon forget that I ever existed."

"Never! Never!" he said in a broken voice.

"Oh yes you will," she replied cheerfully. "Time is a wonderful consoler—besides, Doctor Nestley, I could never have married you, for though you did not then, you know now—I am going to marry Mr. Blake."

"And what difference will that make to you?" he asked mockingly, lifting his dull eyes to her earnest face.

"I do not understand you," she said coldly, drawing back.

"Then I can easily explain," replied the young man quickly, "the only difference will be this—you love him, you do not love me—for the rest both Reginald Blake—or shall I call him Garsworth?—and myself will be equal in all else."

"You are talking wildly," said Una in an icy tone, "so I shall leave you—permit me to pass, if you please?"

"Not till I have had my say," he retorted, his eyes growing bright. "I can wring your proud heart now as you wrung mine then. I saw your look of horror when you looked at me and saw how low I had fallen through drink—in the same way you will look upon your lover when he returns from the guardianship of Basil Beaumont."

Una gave a cry of alarm, and reeled against the stone parapet of the bridge for support, while a cold hand seemed to clutch at her heart.

"You have heard of those devils of old who tempted mankind," went on Nestley rapidly. "Yes, you have heard such stories and thought them pious fictions of Catholicism—but it is true, quite true. There are devils of like sort in our midst even now, and Basil Beaumont is one. I knew him in London five years ago when I was a young man just starting in life. I had no vices, I had great talents, I was devoted to my profession and all seemed to promise a fair life. But Beaumont came, devil that he is, in the guise of an angel of light, and ruined me. He beguiled me with his wheedling tongue and specious manners into believing in him. Having gained my confidence he led me to gamble and drink until I sank so low that even he forsook me —yes, forsook the man he had ruined. It was when his fatal influence was withdrawn that I began to recover. I took the pledge, left London and its fascinations and plunged into hard work. For five years I never touched alcohol and things seemed going well with me once more—but I came down here and met him again. I resisted his persuasions for a long time, but on the day you rejected me I was worn out with watching by the bedside of the Squire, and sick with disappointment; he persuaded me to take a glass of wine—it was followed by another—and then—I need not go on, but next morning I found I had lost my self-respect. I gave way to despair, there seemed no hope for me, and now see what I am, and all through Basil Beaumont —I have lost my good name—my money— my position—everything—everything in the world."

Sick with horror Una tried to speak, but could only look at him with white lips and a terrified face. Seeing her alarm he resumed his discourse but in a somewhat milder fashion.

"Your lover has gone to London, and Beaumont is with him. He is the possessor of money. Beaumont will want to handle that money; to do so he will reduce Reginald Blake to a mere cypher. Do you know how he will do it? I will tell you. By fast living—he will reduce your lover to the abject condition I was in, and through him squander the Garsworth money. It does not matter how high Reginald Blake's principles may be, how pure he desires to live, how temperate he may have been, he is in the power of Basil Beaumont, and, little by little, will be dragged down to the lowest depths of degradation and despair."

"No, no!" she cried, wildly, "it cannot be!"

"It will be, I tell you—I know Beaumont, you do not—if you would save your lover, get him out of the clutches of that devil, or

he will become an object of horror to you
as I am."

He turned away with a look of despair,
and crossing the bridge on to the common,
slouched along the muddy road without
casting a glance back, while Una, with pale
face and tightly-clenched hands, gazed after
him with mute agony in her eyes.

"Oh, great Heaven!" she moaned,
lifting up her wan face to the grey sky, "if
this should be true—it must be true—I can
see he is speaking the truth! Reginald to
sink to that—no, no! I'll go and see the
vicar. I will tell him all—all! We must
save him before it is too late!"

With feverish impatience she began to
walk down the street on her way to the
vicarage, intent only on finding some means
of saving the man she loved.

And the man who had no woman to save
him slouched wearily along the road—a
lonely, desolate figure, with only the grey

sky above and the grey earth below, with
no hope, no peace, no love awaiting, but
only the blank, black shadow of approaching
sorrow brooding over his life with sombre
wings.

CHAPTER III.

A MOTHER'S AFFECTION.

Niobe. From cruel Phœbus all my children fly.
Chorus. Fly then, oh Queen, else will they bring thee
           harm.
Niobe. What evil counsel is upon thy tongue?
Chorus. The counsel that would save thee from thyself.
Niobe. A mother's love should thus protect her child.
Chorus. From such protection cometh death to thee.
Niobe. Death will be welcome if it cometh thus
    For naught thou knowest of true motherhood
    Thinking that fear of death will drive me hence
    To leave mine offspring to Phœbean darts.

THE next day was Sunday, and during the night there was a heavy fall of snow, so the Garsworth folk were not a little astonished, upon rising in the morning, to find the ground white, and the sky of a dull, leaden colour. Una had seen the vicar, and, in consequence of the interview she had with him, had written a letter to

Reginald, which she was enclosing in an envelope when Patience Allerby entered in order to clear away the breakfast-things. She saw that Una had been writing to Reginald, and a gleam of interest crossed her stolid face as she looked eagerly at her mistress. Una guessed her thoughts, and. knowing the woman's deep interest in Reginald, arising, as she thought, from the fact of Patience being his nurse, spoke to her on the subject.

"I am writing to Mr. Blake," she said, closing the envelope, "as I am anxious for him to return to Garsworth."

"He is all right, is he not, Miss Una?" asked Patience anxiously.

"Oh, yes, I think so," replied Una, doubtfully, "but I have been talking with the vicar, and he agrees with me that it is dangerous for Reginald to be in London."

"Danger—from whom?"

"Mr. Beaumont."

"Mr. Beaumont!" echoed Patience, in a harsh voice. "What has he been doing to my boy?"

Una looked at her in astonishment, for the whole face of the woman seemed transformed, and instead of wearing its usual calm expression it was convulsed with stormy passions. For once the mask had fallen off, and Una recognised the terrible force of character hidden under this woman's placid exterior. The housekeeper also felt that she had betrayed herself and strove to recover her lost ground by an explanation.

"I beg your pardon, Miss Una, if I speak angrily," she said feverishly, "but remember I was Mr. Blake's nurse, and he is the only being I care about in this world— if harm happened to him I would never forgive myself."

"I hope there is no chance of harm happening to him," replied Una gently, "but he is in London with Mr. Beaumont, and from what Dr. Nestley told me about that gentleman I don't think he is a good companion for Reginald."

"Dr. Nestley," said Patience thoughtfully, "I was not aware Dr. Nestley had met Mr. Beaumont before."

"Yes, I believe they met in London," replied Una, and proceeded to direct the envelope, while Patience thinking over what she had heard left the room.

When she had finished all her work for the day she retired to her room in order to think over the conversation. Judging from what Miss Challoner had told her Beaumont was trying to ruin Reginald, and she guessed his motive for doing so. Patience was well enough acquainted with the artist to know that he did nothing without an object, and as he had placed Blake in receipt of ten thousand a year, she foresaw that his next step would be to handle it. As he could only do this through Reginald he was trying to get the boy completely into his power in order to do what he pleased. As to Dr. Nestley's remarks, he evidently knew something about Beaumont's former life, and Patience after some thought came to the decision that she would call upon Dr. Nestley that afternoon and find out all he knew about him.

Having taken this resolution she put on her things and went out, after telling Jellicks she would come back again in about two or three hours.

Outside, the snow had ceased to fall, and all the cold tints and wretched appearance of the landscape were hidden under a pure white covering. The bare branches of the trees were all laden with powdery snow, which was shaken down in white flakes at every breath of wind. The long lines of thorny hedges ran along the white surface in black lines, and here and there tall,

gaunt trees stood up in startling contrast
of colour. Patience, however, saw none of
the beauties of winter, but trudged slowly
along the half-obliterated road and thought
of the perils to which Reginald was being
exposed by his own father.

Then she crossed the bridge, and, glancing over the side, saw the leaden-coloured
water sweeping drearily between the white
banks, the sloping roof of the church
covered with whiteness like an altar covered
by the sacramental cloth ; the heavy grey
stones of the tower, and beyond the tall red
chimneys of the vicarage, making a cheerful spot of bright colour against the bluish
sky.

She knew that Nestley was stopping at
" The House of Good Living," so went
straight there and asked for him, where-
upon she was shown into the parlour,
before the fire of which was seated the
unhappy young man, looking more worn

out and haggard than ever. He started to his feet when he saw Patience and stared anxiously at her, speaking the thought that was uppermost in his mind :

"Is Miss Una ill?" he asked, thinking she had come for his professional services.

"No, sir," replied Patience sitting down and throwing back her veil, "Miss Una is quite well—I have come to see you on my own business."

"Are you ill?" he asked wearily, resuming his seat and leaning his head upon his hand, "what is the matter with you?"

"Nothing at all," she answered coldly. "My health is all right, but I wish to speak to you about Mr. Beaumont."

Dr. Nestley looked at her in surprise, with a bitter smile on his lips.

"What, you too?" he said derisively, "are you another of his victims?"

"No—I am not his victim—but, as you know, I am the nurse of Mr. Blake, who lately succeeded to the property, and as he is now in London with Mr. Beaumont I want to hear from your own lips what danger you think there is in such companionship."

"What can I say?"

"Everything; you told Miss Una your story yesterday and she said something about it to me——"

"Betrayed my confidence?"

"Nothing of the sort, sir, she merely said you did not consider Mr. Beaumont a good companion for a young man, nothing more —is it true?"

"Perfectly true. I know what Beaumont is from my own experience of him—he will drag Reginald Blake down to the lowest depths of degradation."

The woman tightened her thin lips ominously.

"I don't think so if I can help it," she said grimly.

" Then if you can help it—if you have
any power over him—take Blake away from
his influence or he will ruin him."

" Are you sure ? "

"Sure," he repeated bitterly, "I know it
only too well to my own cost, God help me !
Basil Beaumont is a devil, and never rests
till he makes his friends as base as himself.
Blake has got money, Beaumont wants that
money, and will let nothing stand in his
way to procure it."

" He had better not set himself up against
me."

" What do you know about him ? "

" More than he cares the world to know."

" Then use that knowledge to keep him
away from Garsworth."

" I don't care if he comes to Garsworth
as long as he leaves my—my boy alone.

" Your boy ? "

" Reginald Blake—I was his nurse—I
will get him to return here, and if he marries

Miss Una I don't think Mr. Beaumont will be able to do much."

"He'll do this much," cried Nestley quickly, "he'll try and prevent the marriage."

"Why?" she asked curtly. "For what reason?"

"The best of all reasons—he loves Una Challoner himself."

Patience arose to her feet with a cry, her face turned to a ghastly pallor.

"You—you—are mad," she gasped, placing her hand on her heart, "it cannot be true."

"It is true, I tell you," said Nestley in a harsh whisper, coming close to her. "Una Challoner would not listen to me because she loves Reginald Blake. Beaumont also loves her and sees Blake is an obstacle in his path, he will remove that obstacle by fair means or foul—but remove it he will—he'll obtain such power over Blake that he will

get him to make a will in his favour, then
—then—you can guess what will follow."

"Oh! but it's horrible—horrible—this
man would never do such a thing."

"I know Basil Beaumont—you don't."

"Don't I!". she cried viciously, turning
round. "I know him only too well—I was
a good woman once!"

"Ah! I thought you were another
victim," said Nestley cynically. "And
what do you propose to do?"

"Do!" she said fiercely. "I will write
him a letter and warn him once and for all
—if he refuses to accept the warning I will
show him no mercy—he must give up all
thought of Una Challoner—she shall marry
Reginald Blake and none other."

"She will never do that while Beaumont
lives—I know she loves Blake, but Beaumont loves her, and what are those two
innocents against his devilish craftiness?"

"He has got to deal with me as well as

with them," she said grandly. "Sooner than Beaumont shall harm a hair of their heads I will end his life and his villainies at the same time."

"You would not kill him?"

"I will do what I say—if he does not accept the warning I send him, his life is in his own hands not mine."

Nestley stood silent with astonishment, while without another word, Patience swept out of the room, and then only did he recover his power of speech.

"Ugh!" he said with a shiver. "I believe she will—but no—Beaumont is a man nothing can harm—devils are sent upon the earth for some purpose, and he is one."

He crouched down over the fire, the red light of which glared upon his face, bringing out all the lines and hollows now stamped on it and making him look very old and grey. Outside, the night was closing in, and he shivered again as the deep voice of the church bell rang through the keen air.

"It's Sunday," he whispered. "Sunday night—I ought to go to church. Church!" he repeated with a dreary laugh, "there's no church for me—between myself and God stands the devil of Drink."

CHAPTER IV.

> Some chance word
> May strike upon an inattentive ear
> And rouse the soul from selfish slumberings,
> To wrestle with a thousand subtle foes
> That would destroy its hope of Paradise.

OUTSIDE the snow fell fast and thick from the dull impenetrable sky, but within the church all was warmth and light. Owing to the primitive civilisation of the village the holy edifice was only illuminated by a few oil lamps, which just sufficed to fill it with shadows. The great arched roof above was completely in darkness, and hanging low down, almost on a level with the pews, the lamps burned with a dull yellow light in the heavy atmosphere. On the communion table four tapers shone like

amber-coloured stars, touching the white
limbs of the Christ hanging on the ebony
cross with fitful lights. A lamp enclosed
in a red globe swung from the centre
of the chancel arch, flaming fiercely
crimson like a red eye glaring out of
the semi-darkness, and on each side of
the pulpit two candles threw a doubtful
glimmer on the open bible. Amid all
this fantasy of shadow and light knelt
the simple villagers with bowed heads,
following, with murmuring voices, the
Lord's Prayer, recited by the vicar.
The confused sound buzzed among the
multitudinous arches, losing itself in
faint echoes amid the great oaken beams,
and then the thunder of the organ rolled
out a melodious amen which died away
in a whisper as, with a rustle, the congregation arose to their feet to make the
responses.

During the singing of the Psalms, the

door at the lower end of the church opened and, heralded by a blast of cold air which made all the lamps flicker, a man stole stealthily to a dark seat and knelt down. This was Duncan Nestley, who, tortured by maddening thoughts and overpowering mental anguish, had come to religion for consolation, now kneeling, with hot dry eyes and clasped hands amid the shadows.

The evening psalm was that magnificent chant wherein David describes Jehovah as coming forth in all his glory, and the choir, really being an excellent one, the rolling verse of the Hebrew poet was well rendered. The thin treble of the boys rang out piercingly shrill through the mystic twilight.

"*He rode upon the cherubims and did fly: he came flying upon the wings of the wind.*"

Then, without pause, the deeper voices of the men thundered out the sublime words:

"*He made darkness his secret place: his pavilion round about him with dark water and thick clouds to cover him.*"

No wonder, as the great volume of sound rang through the church, the heart of the unhappy man was filled with fear.

This terrible Deity who came forth in such appalling splendour was his enemy, this awful Jehovah of the Hebrews, in whose hand flashed the sword of vengeance, was his merciless judge, and kneeling there with tightly clenched hands he felt crushed to the earth by the fierce denunciations thundered forth by the choir. But then a change came over the terrible vehemence of the music.

and sweet as a silver trumpet rang out the proclamation :

" The Lord liveth, and blessed be my strong helper and praised be the God of my salvation."

There was mercy then—this unknown Splendour whose terrors had been shadowed forth with such grandeur had pity as well as vengeance ; a dull feeling of exhaustion stole over him as the psalm ended with the promise of mercy, and his dry lips moved mutely as though to join in the final " Glory be to the Father."

He did not rise from his knees, but still in a posture of abject supplication heard, as in a dream, the reading of the lessons and the sweet kindly music of the hymns. It was only when the vicar, tall and stately in his white surplice, mounted the pulpit and gave out the text, that he stirred. With a weary sigh he arose and sat down in the pew, utterly exhausted by the conflicting emotions roused within him by the music, but the words of the text given out by the resonant voice of Dr. Larcher seemed to convey some comfort to his despairing soul.

" *Then they cry unto the Lord in their trouble and He saveth them out of their distresses.*"

He listened to the sermon idly at first, but soon found, to his surprise, that he was following the words of the preacher with close attention. Dr. Larcher was no golden-mouthed Chrysostom by any manner of means, but he preached a plain, homely sermon, eminently adapted to the simple congregation of which he was pastor. Never for a moment did he lose himself amid abstruse theological arguments which they could not have understood, but told them practical truths in vigorous Saxon, the meaning of which no one could fail to grasp.

" For, my brethren, when a man is at the lowest depths of despair it is then that he first calls upon the name of the Lord. In time of peace and plenty, when our friends are around us and our coffers are full, we are alas too apt to forget that all these benefits come from the Almighty, and thus at times neglect to thank Him for His many mercies. But when the clouds of adversity gather around us, when the loved ones sink into the grave, when our worldly wealth disappears like snow, when our name becomes a by-word of scorn and reproach, it is then that we turn to God for that help which is denied to us by man. And does he ever refuse to aid us?—No!— In the words of the Psalmist, ' Cast thy

34*

burden upon the Lord and He shall sustain thee'—to the heart that is truly contrite He gives peace and help in time of need; none so low but that He will not hear and grant their prayers if made from the heart. It is not to the terrible Jehovah of the Jewish nation, with pomp and pride of sacrifices and blowing of silver trumpets, that we of later generations appeal. No, since the coming of our dear Lord, who forms the link between most high heaven and lowly earth, we offer up humble prayers to Him in solitude, and He, the mild and merciful Father of us all, dries the tears from our eyes and takes the sorrows from our hearts. If a man be weak and would commit sin let him call upon the Lord and he will be strengthened—if the temptations to which he has been exposed have been too heavy for his bearing and he has succumbed, let him implore mercy of the Almighty and he shall surely find it. Alas! how often do *we find unforgiveness in men. Forgetting the words of Christ, 'Forgive us our trespasses as we forgive them that trespass against us,' they turn their faces away and leave us abased in the dust, but Christ lifts us from that position of humiliation with comforting words, 'Arise poor sinner, and thy sins be forgiven thee, for to this end did I come into the world.' If there be any one of you present who has sinned let him repent this night and he will find the peace of God which passeth all understanding. If he be weak, God will give him strength to conquer; if he be in despair, God will give him hope of pardon. Pray—pray unceasingly, for it is by prayer alone that our weak voices can reach the ear of the eternal Father."*

Nestley waited to hear no more, but with a stifled cry of anguish fled from the church into the cold, white world outside.

Stumbling over the tombstones, through the blinding snow—now falling in thick flakes—he soon found himself in the open street, and urged by some mad impulse, he knew not what, he sped wildly onward through the market-place, over the bridge and on to the trackless common. With clenched teeth and wild, staring eyes he made head against the storm that was sweeping along. His feet made no sound on the yielding snow and he glided along like an unquiet ghost, the burning words of the sermon ringing in his ears.

He was in the lowest depths of despair and all men had turned their faces from him ; he would call upon the Lord to help him—but would God attend ?—surely He would—What were the words of the text ?

"Then they cry unto the Lord in their trouble and He saveth them out of their distresses."

He also would cry and the Lord would save him from the terrible agony he was enduring. He would kneel down there and then in the snow and call upon this unseen God, pavilioned in the terrible splendour of encircling clouds to aid him.

" God ! Help me ! "

No answer save the whistling of the wind and the soft sound of the snow sweeping past, caressing his cold face with delicate touch.

" God ! show me how to be saved."

Nothing, nothing, only the black sky above, the white earth below, and himself, between the two, a reckless, despairing man holding up his helpless hands.

" Our Father which art in heaven———"

How sweet those words sounded ; he had surely heard them at his mother's knee— then he was an innocent child, but now !

Oh God, the evil life he had lived since then!

" God! God!—pity and save! "

It was getting quite warm now and he felt drowsy; if he slept for a while he would then awake and ask God once more to save him; but no, if he fell asleep in the snow he would never awake again, for this treacherous snow would slay him with cold embraces. He would die—die. Ah! he could not die, even though lulled to sleep by the siren voice, and soft caressing of the snow-queen; life was sweet, so he would fight to retain it.

A long struggle and he was on his feet; the road! where was the road? he could not see it. Never mind, the snow and wind were at his back, he would walk on till he came to the bridge, then he would be in safety. Oh, the weary, weary miles —half dazed, half mad, he staggered on,

reeling like a drunken man. Would the
road never come to an end? Oh this
incessant whirl of snow-flakes that he was
in; it was the dance of death, and he was
the dancer.

Quicker and quicker fell the flakes on
the white common and over the dark surface of the Gar, but no figure was struggling along now; no, it was lying upon the
bridge, a disordered heap of black clothing,
which the snow was rapidly hiding beneath
its soft white mantle.

Over the bridge comes the horse and gig
of a sturdy farmer who has to cross the
wild white waste beyond to reach home,
and the sturdy farmer himself with his
buxom wife beside him drives the wise old
horse. Suddenly the old horse shies at the
figure lying in the snow—a start on the
part of the farmer and his wife — then
exclamations and calls for help, black
figures come gliding over the snow like

shadows, and kindly hands raise Duncan Nestley from his deadly resting-place.

They take him to the inn, place him before a roaring fire, force some hot brandy between his blue lips, and rub his frozen limbs to bring back the circulation of the chill blood.

Dead! no, not dead! he opens his eyes. In them there is no intelligence, only a vacant stare—he babbles a few words and then falls back in a faint.

Delirious, yes, and delirious for many a long day, poor soul.

CHAPTER V.

LONDON.

London is the candle which, ever attracting country moths by its feverish glare destroys them remorselessly in its cruel flame.

REGINALD BLAKE was not enjoying himself very much in town owing to his disturbed state of mind. For years he had pictured to himself the marvellous city and his life therein; how he would one day find himself a denizen of the great metropolis, eager to win fame and fortune by the magic of his voice, how he would delight in leading the ambitious, half Bohemian, wholly delightful existence of a singer, and how he would be able to wander about the streets and see the brilliant life of the mighty city with its restless activity and ardent strivings after wealth, fame and novelty.

Grey Westminster Abbey, noble St. Paul's, the enormous pile of the Parliament House, the golden-topped column of the Monument, he would see all these, with their wealth of historical, religious and artistic associations. He would tread the very streets over whose stones wandered proud poverty-stricken Chatterton, courtly Addison and ponderous Dr. Johnson; he would find the picturesque alleys, houses and roads described in the fascinating pages of Dickens, and he would stray about the sacred purlieus of Drury Lane, haunted by the stately shades of Wilkes, of Siddons, of Bracegirdle, and David Garrick. Good heavens, what innumerable fantastic castles did he not build in Cloud Cuckoo Land about the unseen glories of London, where every street and stone was redolent of the glorious history of England from Plantagenet to Guelph.

Oh, beautiful castles of Cloudland, how

rapidly did their gorgeousness disappear from his fancy before the disenchanting touch of chilling reality. He was indeed in London, but alas it was not the magic London of his dreams, this enormous assemblage of houses through which flowed a melancholy grey river and over which hung a dismal dark cloud of smoke and fog. The London of romance and the London of reality were two very different things, yet the disenchantment of this dreaming youth was not wholly due to the prosaic appearance of the city itself but rather to the gloom and depression of his spirits.

The recollection of how his wealth had come to him weighed heavily on his mind, causing him to view all things in a most dismal manner, and tortured his sensitive disposition with irritating thoughts and maddening delusions. In vain he tried hard to shake off this

gloomy feeling and enjoy the many-
coloured life of the great city; in vain
he told himself that the accident of his
birth was no fault of his own and in
vain he strove to take pleasure in the
society of the men and women to whom
he had been introduced by Basil Beaumont. It was all useless, for a dark
cloud of bitterness and distrust seemed
to settle upon the joyousness of his life
which led him to view everything with
jaundiced eyes. He felt that he had lost
the adolescent zest for life as Donatello
must have done after he had stained his
hands with blood, and although he had
youth, talent, good looks, and wealth,
yet all these delightful gifts of the
fairies were neutralized by the fatal gift
of dishonour bestowed upon him by the
malignant beldame who had proved herself the evil genius of his life.

As soon as the business connected

with the Garsworth estate was properly completed and he had been fully recognized as the heir of the old squire, Bolby considering that he had done his duty, left the young man and his friend Dick pretty well to their own devices. Dick enjoyed everything with the inexhaustible appetite of youth, but Reginald took his pleasures, such as they were, in a listless manner, which showed how completely he had lost all capabilities of enjoyment.

Mr. Pemberton had been rather irritated by the prosaic life they led when in the leading strings of Mr. Bolby, whose ideas of amusement were of the most primitive nature, rarely extending beyond an afternoon at the Zoo or a night at Madame Tussaud's or the Egyptian Hall. The only thing Dick saw in Mr. Bolby's ideas of life, which he considered at all meritorious were the ex-

cellent dinners which the little lawyer
gave them, but Dick in his flying visits to
the metropolis had tasted of the Tree of
Knowledge beneath whose shade were the
music halls and the burlesque theatres,
so he was anxious to go to such-like
places for his amusement.

When they left Mr. Bolby, therefore,
and were comfortably established in a
quiet hotel in Jermyn Street, Dick seeing that Reginald was absolutely indif-
ferent as to where he went, or what he
did, took the whole arrangement of their
London life into his own hands and
succeeded in going to a good many
places which would have terribly shocked
the vicar had he known. Not that such
forbidden pleasures did them much harm,
for both lads were extremely sensible for
their age, still Dick finding himself able,
through Reginald's generosity, to spend
a good deal of money, took his friend

and himself to sundry shady places of which they might just as well have been ignorant. But Nemesis soon came down upon the unhappy Richard, and just as he was developing into a fair specimen of a man about town his bachelor uncle at Folkestone wrote him a letter asking him to come down on a visit, and as Dick was supposed to be his bachelor uncle's heir, he had to leave London, much to his own disgust and to the regret of Reginald, who missed his lively friend every hour of the day.

He still stayed in town, however, but as he knew no one, his existence was to say the least extremely dull. Reginald was essentially of a social nature and wanted someone to whom he could talk, therefore he was not sorry when one day Basil Beaumont, who had been waiting for the departure of Dick, called upon him and henceforth constituted himself his bear leader. As they had seen nothing of the artist since their arrival, Dick had never thought of telling Reginald his mistrust of the fascinating Beaumont, so the young man, remembering the artist's kindness about his probable career ·as a singer, felt very friendly towards him and was quite prepared to accept his offer of companionship as the outcome of a kindly disposition and not the result of a carefully calculated scheme.

A more dangerous companion for a young man in a depressed state of mind than Beaumont could hardly be imagined, for he led Reginald to plunge into riotous pleasures for the sake of distraction, from which he would have otherwise recoiled. Having an eminently refined mind, and a delight in cultured company, had he been thoroughly healthy he would never have been drawn by this modern Mephistopheles into the vortex of frenzied pleasure in which his days and nights were now engulfed. But, being in a morbid state of mind, he brooded eternally over the presumed stigma attached to his name until it became a perfect nightmare to him. He thought that everyone knew his miserable story and despised him for the anomalous position he now occupied, so, in a mad spirit of bravado, he became quite reckless, and determined to defy the world which his sensitive spirit imagined to be sneering at him as a bastard. Terrible to relate, in spite of the relationship existing between them, Beaumont, who should have prevented the young man from falling into such an unhealthy state of mind, rather encouraged his gloomy fits than otherwise, as he thought it would give him a greater hold than ever over his son, so deliber-

35*

ately led the unhappy young man on to ruin—ruin, not of his fortune or position, but of his physical and moral nature.

In his best days, the circle of Beaumont's acquaintances had not been a very large or reputable one, but now it was smaller and worse than ever; nevertheless, he introduced the young master of Garsworth Grange to his friends, whose manners, generally speaking, were as polished as their morals were bad. Broken down professional men, played-out lords, ruined gentlemen of fortune, shady hangers-on of society; these were the daily associates of Reginald Blake, until his mind, eminently calculated to receive impressions, began to be corrupted. The society of hawks is rather a dangerous thing for doves, and this poor unsophisticated dove was of far too guileless a nature to mistrust the birds

of prey by which he found himself sur-
rounded, though to be sure, his natural
instincts of right and wrong saved him
from many a pitfall.

Not that the hawks around him did
any harm to his pecuniary position, for
Beaumont was too selfish to allow any-
one to have the plucking of this well-
feathered pigeon save himself, and there
being an unwritten code of honour even
among hawks, the young man was left
entirely to the tender mercies of his
evil-minded Mentor. Nevertheless, the
long nights of play, the wiles of women
whose beauty did not redeem their
frailty, and the constant life of excite-
ment passed under the feverish glare of
the gaslight, soon destroyed the fresh
healthy feeling of youth which Reginald
Blake had possessed during the quiet
years of his country life.

When at times his better feelings pre-

vailed, and he would have fled this unhealthy life of bitter-tasting pleasures,
Beaumont was always at his elbow with
some new device wherewith to beguile
him to destruction.   Blake was not a
weak-minded man by any means, still he
was young and impressionable, and the
sudden change from the poverty and
quiet living of Garsworth, to the opulent,
brilliant life of London, threw him off
his moral balance.

No doubt he should have bravely resisted the allurements of sin, and the
shallow frivolities to which he yielded
with the apathy of despair, but, in the
Armida-like gardens of London, the
keenest eyes are blinded, the acutest
senses are bewildered, and dazed by the
hubbub and brilliance around him, the
victim falls only too easily into the snares
hidden below the splendid pageant.

One thing, however, Reginald stoutly

resisted, and that was the temptation to drink—he played nap and baccarat, losing comparatively large sums thereat, mixed in the society of women who lured him onward to destruction with siren voices, but in spite of Beaumont's insidious enticements he never took more wine than was good for him, and this temperance was in a certain measure a guard against the fatal influence of his otherwise foolish life. However, Beaumont was not impatient, as he knew from experience the effect of time in wearing away good resolutions, and waited calmly until some lucky chance should enable him to put a finishing stroke to the ruin of his unhappy son.

It seems almost incredible that such a man as Basil Beaumont, from whom not even his own flesh and blood was safe, could exist; but unhappily, he is only one of the many men in whom all natural love and affection is entirely destroyed by the vicious, feverish life which they lead.

Behold, therefore, this unhappy country moth lured to destruction by the garish glitter of the lights of London beneath which sat the fatal Circe of pleasure, with rose-crowned hair and wine-filled cup. Around her moved the splendid throng of pleasure seekers, dancing, singing, eating and drinking, taking no heed of the morrow in the evil joy of the present ; but, below this glittering maelstrom of vice and rascality, were the rose-hidden pitfalls into which every moment sank some gay reveller, his dying cry of despair drowned in the riotous crowd dancing gaily over his unseen grave.

CHAPTER VI.

CIRCE'S CUP.

In her cup the red wine glows,
Fragrant as the blushing rose ;
Cure of sorrows, cure of woes,
   From it thou wilt win.
Ah ! but Circe's cup deceives,
Evil spell its magic weaves,
To the fool who drinks—it leaves
   The bitterness of sin.

ONE night Reginald and Beaumont were comfortably seated over their cigarettes and coffee in the smoking-room of the hotel, talking in a desultory kind of way about the news of the day, when Blake suddenly made a remark quite foreign to the conversation.

"I often wonder why you have never married, Beaumont," he said idly.

The artist shrugged his shoulders.

"It's not difficult to answer," he replied lightly. "I have never met any woman I particularly cared about."

"Wouldn't you like to be married?" asked Reginald.

"Humph! that depends. I'm afraid I'm past the age of cultivating the domestic virtues. I am a cosmopolitan—a wanderer —no home would be pleasant to me for any length of time."

"But why don't you settle down?"

"Because the age of miracles is past. I'm one of those men who never know in what land they will lay their bones. No, no! I'm sadly afraid the domestic tea-urn and family circle are not for me."

It was curious to hear this man talk in such a cynical strain to his own son, but then Beaumont had been so long apart from his offspring that he almost regarded him as a stranger, and therefore spoke to him as such.

"I think you would be much happier married," observed Reginald.

"No doubt. You judge me by yourself. When you get married to Miss Challoner and settle down, your life will be a paradise, because long training has rendered you admirably suited to a domestic life. But I —ouf!—I would weary of the best woman in the world"

"What a curious man you are, Beaumont," said Blake, looking at him in a puzzled manner. "This life of yours in Town appears to me so unsatisfying. Everyone is on the move. Never a moment for rest or reflection, a constant striving after pleasure, and when that pleasure is gained, what is it but Dead Sea fruit? Now, on the other hand, I cannot imagine a more delightful life than one in the country. When I marry Una I will live at Garsworth Grange, bring up my children, if I am happy enough to become a father, take an interest in the dear old village, and enjoy my whole existence in a leisurely, pleasant manner, which will give me far more enduring enjoyment than this rapid frivolous town life."

"Your instincts are quite those of a patriarchal age," said Beaumont, with a scarcely concealed sneer, "but of course I can hardly wonder at that. Many years of a highly artificial civilisation have given me a distaste for your beau ideal of life, while the simplicity of your training has unfitted you for the gas and glitter of London. A man brought up on roast beef does not care for truffles, though, to be sure, roast beef is the more healthy of the two."

Reginald laughed at this extraordinary manner of arguing, but did not pursue the subject, and shortly afterwards the pair were whirling along in a hansom to the Totahoop Music Hall.

This establishment, which took its extra-

ordinary name from an eminent comedian
who first opened it as a place of entertain-
ment, was one of the largest, handsomest,
and most patronised music halls in town.
It stood at one side of a large square and
had a palatial appearance with its flight of
marble steps, its enormous folding-doors
and the view they afforded when open of
tropical trees, nude white statues and
gorgeous hangings of blue plush, all of
which looked brilliant under the powerful
radiance of the electric lights.

When the two gentlemen arrived the
promenade was quite full of men and
women, some talking loudly, others attending to the performance, and many crowd-
ing around the marble-topped counters of
the various bars from which smiling bar-
maids dispensed cooling beverages. The
house was quite full and comparatively
quiet, for the ballet of *The Lorelei* was
now being danced, and the stage was

filled with multitudes of pretty girls in costumes of pale green glittering with silver scales, who were swaying to and fro to a swinging waltz rhythm played by the orchestra.

"This is a very good ballet," observed Beaumont, as they took their seats in a private box, "both the scenery and the dances are excellent. Have a drink?"

"No, thank you," replied Blake listlessly, taking off his cloak, "I prefer watching the ballet."

He leaned out of the box and was soon deeply interested in the pantomimic action on the stage, while Beaumont swept the glittering horseshoe with his opera-glass to see if he could espy a friend. Very shortly he saw a man with whom he was well acquainted, and left the box with a muttered apology, while Reginald, absorbed in the ballet, took no notice of his departure.

Veils of pale green gauze were falling
like a curtain in front of the stage, which
was flooded with an emerald light, and
away at the back could be seen the Sea
Palace of the Lorelei, above which undu-
lated the blue waves of the ocean. The
daring young knight in silver armour was
standing like a statue in the centre of the
stage, and round him the nymphs, linked
hand in hand, were wreathing in mysterious
evolutions, growing slower and slower till
they all paused, grouped in graceful atti-,
tudes like living statues. A strange low
chord from the orchestra, and then there
stole forth a weird, subtle melody that
seemed to possess a snake-like fascination
as it arose and fell with shrill sounds of
clarionet and violin. A sudden ripple as
of silver bells, and the fatal Rhine nymph
glided on to the stage from a huge shell
placed far back in the restless green water.
Then there was a dance of fascination,

in which the knight resisted the allurements of the Lorelei, but the sleeping nymphs also awoke and re-commenced their dreamy dance, while through the swing and beat of the band there stole the strange wild piping of the *Lorelei motif*. At last the knight yielded, there was a storm of somewhat discordant music, and all the evil things of ocean came trooping on to the stage, dashing at length into a mad galop as they surged and rolled round the knight, now captive in the arms of the siren. A thick darkness spread over the scene, and when the light broke again the ocean halls had vanished and a merry crowd of peasants were dancing on a fair lawn to the piping of a shepherd.

Reginald did not like this latter scene so much, as it lacked the mysterious enticement of the former, and felt rather dis appointed, but he was quite repaid by the last scene of the ballet, which represented

the fatal Lorelei rock amid turbid waters
under the pale light of the moon.

On the shore wandered the spell-
enchained knight, and Blake thought of
Heine's ballad, with its foreboding beginning,

" Ich weiss nicht was soll es bedeuten,"

as the mysterious melody of the Lorelei
began to once more steal from amid the
sombre music of the orchestra. Lonely is
the knight, for he loves naught on earth
while the water witch has power over him.
Shriller and shriller arose the melody, and
suddenly a white blaze of electric light
envelopes the rock, upon which stands the
siren, combing her marvellous locks of
gold.

With mystic gestures she beckons the
knight ; he launches a boat, and the waves
rise white and threatening amid a storm of
music from the orchestra, while overhead
the thunder rolls and the lightning flashes.

The boat reaches the rock, strikes, and in a
moment the knight is struggling in the
water with hands stretched out imploringly
to the Water Witch.   Darkness once more,
then again the emerald light shines, showing the Halls of the Lorelei, who stands
over the dead body of the knight, while
around swing the river nymphs with floating hair and waving hands, then the shrill
piping of the Lorelei *motif* sounds once
more and the curtain falls.

"Well, what do you think of the ballet?"
asked Beaumont, who had returned to the
box and was watching with keen interest
the dreamy look upon the young man's
face.

"I think it is charming," replied
Reginald, in whose head the mysterious
melody of the Lorelei was still ringing,
" but what a fool that knight was."

"Ah, do you think so?" rejoined the
artist, lightly.   "There I do not agree with

you. Many a man has had his life wrecked
by listening to the music of the Sea Witch.
The legend of the Lorelei is simply an
allegory of life."

"So is the legend of the Sirens, I
suppose," said Blake listlessly.

"Of course, the man who is drawn away
from Nature by the alluring voice of the
world always loses his happiness and
genius."

"I don't think much of your world's
singing," retorted Blake, a trifle cynically.
"It would never allure me."

"It's alluring you now," thought Beaumont, although he did not say so, but
merely remarked, "Too much of modern
sentimentality about it, perhaps, or you
think the world's voice pipes too vulgar a
ditty. There I agree with you, but, unfortunately, in this age we vulgarise everything; we drag forth the lovely mysterious
dreams of mediævalism from their en-

36*

chanted twilights into the broad blaze of
day and then reject them in disgust because
we are disillusionized.   Ah, bah! the world
of to-day, which reduces everything to
plain figures, always puts me in mind of a
child spoiling a drum to find out what's
inside."

"Unpleasant, but true."

"The truth is always unpleasant, my
friend, that is why people so seldom tell it,"
said Beaumont;   "but listen to this recitation.   It's the best thing of the evening."

. The reciter was a celebrated actress who
had been induced to appear upon the
music-hall platform by way of an experiment, to see if the ordinary audience of
such a place would take to the higher
form of art as exemplified by the recitation.

Simply dressed, with no scenic effect,
but only her wonderful voice and strong

dramatic instinct to rely on, the lady recited a touching little piece about a dying woman, and it was truly wonderful the effect it had upon the pleasure-loving audience. In spite of the attractions of comic songs, of pretty girls, of grotesque tumblers, and of daring gymnasts, the whole body of men and women yielded to the spell of the recitation. The poem was full of human nature, and the intensity of the reciter's voice carried the pathos of the pitiful little story home to everyone. The intense humanity of the tale, declaimed in a most dramatic way by an artist, came like a breath of cool mountain air into the perfumed, close atmosphere of a ball-room, and the storm of applause which broke forth at the conclusion of the recitation showed how powerful genius is to move even the most *blasé* of humanity.

"That is a step in the right direction," said Beaumont as he left the music-hall with Reginald, "everyone prophesied failure for such an experiment, but you see the voice of the heart can always reach the heart. There is more culture even among music-hall audiences than we give them credit for."

"I don't think it's a question of culture at all," replied Blake, bluntly; "that simple story declaimed in such a way would appeal to the lowest audience in Whitechapel."

"I daresay you are right," answered Beaumont idly, "a touch of nature makes the whole world akin. I think it was Shakespeare who made that remark— wonderfully wise man—I should like to have seen him write a drama on the complex civilization of to-day."

"Our dramatists of to-day do their best."

"No doubt, but they write on such frivolous subjects. If they took up a broad

question of the time and placed it before us
in the form of a play, they might evolve a
new style of drama fitted to be handed
down to posterity ; but when they concern
themselves only with the drama of little
things, their ideas are as ephemeral as their
plays.   No, this is only the age of scientific
discovery, not the time of poetic imagin-
ings."

Thus talking, they strolled along the
crowded streets, and turned into a supper-
room, where they had a comfortable meal.
Beaumont tried to induce Reginald to come
with him to his club, and have a game of
cards, but the young man, haunted by the
subtle melody of the Lorelei did not feel
inclined for the green table, so bidding the
artist good-night, stepped into a hansom,
and was driven back to his hotel.

All through his sleep that night, the shrill
music rang in his brain, and he dreamed
constantly of the woman with the fatal

beauty, who, sitting on her rock, lured men to destruction.

Did no warning voice whisper the meaning of his dreams, how London, with siren music, was enticing him onward to her cruel pitfalls hidden by roses? No! Apparently good genius had forsaken him, and he was now in the jaws of danger, without a single hand being stretched out to save him from the cruel rocks concealed under the whirling foam, above which the Lorelei sang her evil song.

CHAPTER VII.

A WORD IN SEASON.

I weary of dances, of songs of the south,
   Of sounds of the viol and lute,
Ah, bitter to find that all things in my mouth
   Taste only of bitter sea fruit.

IT was now two months since Reginald had come to London, and he was beginning to get very wearied of the exhausting life he was leading. He half determined to leave town and return home again, but was still undecided, when he received a letter from Una which confirmed his resolution.

Outside the fog was thick and yellow, enveloping the shivering houses in a solid dingy mist, which made everything look ineffably dreary. Along the streets and in the houses gas was burning with an unwilling look, as if it knew it had no right to be lighted during the day. Day!—good heavens, was this semi-twilight the day, with the heavy fog lowering down on the streets, through which the cabs and 'busses crept along in a cautious and stealthy manner? Was that dull red ball, which appeared to give neither light nor heat, the glorious sun? And the atmosphere; a chilling clammy air, which insinuated itself everywhere, making the flesh creep as though at the touch of a repulsive serpent. Assuredly this siren London, so enticing at night, under the glare of countless lamps, was not a pleasant spectacle in the morning, and the smiling rose-wreathed Circe of the evening was changed to a haggard unkempt hag with worn face and dreary eyes.

Reginald was seated at the breakfast table, but the food before him was untouched, as he now felt no appetite, but sat listlessly back in his chair, reading Una's letter, which had just arrived. She was anxious for him to return to Garsworth, and it was this portion of the letter which touched Blake with a certain amount of remorse.

" *You can have no idea how I miss you, Reginald, and every day you are absent seems to part us further from one another. The business which took you up to London must surely be completed by this time, so if you love me, as I know you do, come back at once to Garsworth, and we will be married as soon as is compatible with decorum after the death of your father. Then we can travel on the Continent for a time, and I being by your side will no longer feel this terrible anxiety for your welfare which now constantly haunts me. Although I know your own instincts will always lead you to do what is right and just, both towards yourself and your friends, yet I dread the influence of that dangerous London, against whose temptations even the strongest*

nature cannot prevail. This is the first re-
quest I have ever made to you, dear Reginald,
and I feel sure you will grant it. So come
back at once to me, and remember I shall count
every moment of time until I see you once
more by my side."

When he came to this part of the letter,
Reginald laid it aside and began to think
over the words Una had written.

Yes!—she was quite right—it was better
for him in every way to go back to Garsworth, and leave this feverish, unreal existence which he was now leading. He would
return once more to the old familiar life,
with its gentle simplicity and pleasant
delights—the rising in the early grey of
the morning, the matutinal run with the
dogs across the breezy common—then, later
on in the day, he would meet Una, and stroll
with her through the quiet village streets,
where everyone knew and loved them both,

from the ancient grandmother basking in the sunshine to the prattling child tottering after them for notice with unsteady gait. No fog—no dreary rattle of cabs—no hoarse cries of news-boy and fish-vendor— but the bright beautiful, blue sky, with the golden sun shining, and a moist keen wind blowing from the distant fen lands, filled with strange cold odours stolen from hidden herbs. And in the evening he would sing to her—sing those charming old ballads of Phyllis and Daphne, and Lady Bell—which he had not sung for so many days—or per- haps they would listen to the ponderous conversation of Dr. Larcher, with its classi- cal flavouring of Horace.

The time would pass by in such innocent pleasures upon rapid wings, until their wedding-day came, with the budding leaves in tree and hedge, and the timid out-peeping of delicate spring flowers. Then the genial old vicar would make them man and wife, in the sacred gloom of the familar church, while the wedding march pealed forth from the organ, and the joy-bells clashed in the ancient Norman tower. Afterwards they would go abroad for some months, and wander through old-world cities, among the treasures of dead ages—returning when they were weary, to lead quiet and useful lives under their own roof-tree, and among the friends of their early days. Yes !—he would go back to Garsworth, and try to realize these delightful dreams, but — Beaumont——

At this moment—as if in answer to his thoughts—a knock came to the door, and Beaumont entered—scattering at once the cloud-built castles in which Reginald's dreamy fancy had been indulging. His quick eye at once saw that the young man had eaten no breakfast—and he laughed gaily as he removed his hat and sat down near the fire.

"Don't feel well this morning?" he said lightly. "What a humbug you are, Blake —a little dissipation should be nothing for a healthy young country fellow like you."

"That's just it," replied Reginald, with some animation, slipping Una's letter into his pocket. "I am a country fellow, accustomed to lead a quiet simple life—and not an artificial existence."

"Oh, you'll soon get used to it."

"No doubt, but I'm not going to make the attempt."

"Oh, indeed!" observed Beaumont, concealing his annoyance. "So you intend to return to that dead-and-alive hole of a Garsworth?"

"Hole, as you think it," replied the young man, with some warmth, "it has been my home for many a long year, and I have grown to love it; besides, you forget —I go back to be married."

"But surely not yet?" objected Beaumont earnestly. "Your father has not been dead very long. Besides, you must have a fling as a bachelor before you become Benedict, the married man."

"I've had enough 'fling,' as you call it," said Reginald, coldly, "and I don't like it—-this incessant high-pressure style of life is not to my taste, so I am going away from it."

"I'm afraid I cannot leave London, just now," said the artist, with a frown, feeling his prey was slipping through his fingers.

Blake looked at him in surprise.

"I do not want you to leave London," he observed, in a dignified manner. "There is no necessity for you to accompany me by any manner of means—you have your own life and your own friends, I have mine, so there is nothing in common between us in any way. You have certainly been very kind, in offering to assist me as a singer, but, as I do not require your assistance now, of course I will not trouble you. No doubt I have taken up a considerable portion of your time since I have been in London, but I am willing to repay any loss you may have sustained in whatever way you suggest."

He looked straight at Beaumont as he spoke; and that gentleman, feeling rather nonplussed by the calm dignity of the young man, had the grace to blush a little, while he rapidly calculated on his next move. His financial affairs were not by any means in ·a flourishing condition at present, and he would have liked to ask Blake to give him some money; but, not judging the time ripe enough to prefer such a request, he temporised in a crafty manner.

" You misunderstand me," he said

smoothly. "What I have done, is out of
pure kindness, and I want no return for
it. If you feel inclined to return to Garsworth, of course you are your own master,
and can do so. Some day, I may run
down to see you, and if I can be of any
assistance to you, in connection with the
management of your estates, of course I
will be only too happy to do what I can."

"Thank you, I will not forget your
offer," replied Reginald, still rather
coldly, for he did not like the masterful
tone adopted by the artist. "And now,
if you will excuse me, I'll go and pack
up my portmanteau."

"Oh, I'll come and see you off, at
Paddington," said Beaumont, cheerily;
"what train are you going by?"

"The mid-day train," answered Blake,
glancing at his watch.

"Then I'll see you on the platform,"
observed Beaumont, rising to his feet and

taking up his hat. "By-the-way, what about your engagements for this week?"

"I'll have to break them—none are very important, and most rather expensive."

Beaumont, biting his lips at this home-thrust, made no reply beyond a careless laugh; and, putting on his hat, left the room with a jaunty air. Once outside, however, his face changed to an expression of deep anger; for his success with Blake, hitherto, had not led him to expect such a calm resistance to his wishes.

"You'll defy me, will you?" he muttered between his teeth, as he walked rapidly along the street. "I'll see about that, my boy—as I put you in possession of the property, I can also take it from you again; and I'll do it, unless you're guided by me. I'll wait till you go back to Garsworth, and follow shortly afterwards. Once you know the truth, and I

37*

don't think you'll be so anxious to get
rid of your best friend. I can leave you
rich—or make you a pauper; so the
whole of your future life is in my hands,
and I'll mould it as I please."

Though he was annoyed at the unexpected display of firmness made by Blake,
he was not alarmed, knowing he held
the strongest hand in the game, and that
Reginald would be forced to yield everything up to him, if he wanted to remain
rich. Still, it was most irritating, for no
one likes the worm to turn, as it is
plainly the duty of the worm to be
trodden upon; and for such a miserable
thing as the worm to resent its fate, is
going in direct opposition to the laws of
Nature. However, there is an exception
to every rule; and in this case Mr.
Beaumont's worm was more daring than
he had any idea of; and, in spite of
being the strongest party, he might well

doubt with whom the victory would ultimately rest.

However, Beaumont's habitual self-command came to his aid, and prevented him showing any irritation, when he stood on the Paddington platform at the window of a smoking carriage, wishing Reginald good-bye.

"I hope you have enjoyed your stay in London," he said heartily.

"So, so," answered Reginald wearily. "I cannot enjoy anything very much, knowing the circumstances of my birth."

"Nonsense! You'll soon forget all about that."

"I don't think [so, unfortunately for myself I have not your happy facility for forgetting."

"Pshaw! You are rich, and gold hides everything."

"From the eyes of the world, yes; but not from a man's own sight—nobody knows but the wearer where the shoe pinches."

"If that is the case, let the wearer smile blandly, and the world will never guess his shoe doesn't fit him—it's your fools, who wear their hearts on their sleeves, that get the worst word of every-one."

"And the wise man who conceals a vicious life gets the praise," said Blake bitterly. "What a delightful world."

"It's the best of all possible worlds," retorted Beaumont cynically. "I agree with M. Voltaire—besides, the world always takes you at your own valuation; smile, and it smiles; frown, and it looks grim; each man is a mirror to another, and gives back the reflection he receives."

"What cold-blooded philosophy."

"No doubt, but a very necessary philosophy," retorted Beaumont in a good-humoured tone; "it's ridiculous to bring the simplicity of Arcady to Rome. France tried it under the Fourteenth Louis, and the experiment ended in the guillotine and the Carmagnole."

The train was now moving off, so he shook hands with the young man through the open window of the carriage.

"Good-bye," said Reginald heartily, "when you come to Garsworth, I'll be glad to see you, my friend."

"Friend," echoed Beaumont with an evil smile, as the long train steamed away, "next time you see me it will be as your master."

CHAPTER VIII.

A VOICE FROM THE PAST.

Only a woman's heart—indeed ;
A sacred thing to you, you say,
To me, a toy, with which to play,
Ah, well, let each hold fast his creed.

What matter should it chance to bleed,
Is it a man's cut finger?—nay,
Only a woman's heart.

On ancient tales your fancies feed,
When woman ruled in saintly way,
But we have changed such things to-day,
For, after all, what use to heed
Only a woman's heart.

SEEING that Reginald had thus escaped him for a time, Mr. Beaumont's temper was none of the sweetest when he arrived back at his chambers. Like most clever men, the artist was very proud of his tact and delicacy in dealing with ingenuous youth, and he felt annoyed with himself lest by failing to skilfully angle for this trout, he should have lost his prize by failing in his diplomacy, and thereby shown too plainly the real reasons he had for his apparently disinterested friendship. So, on arrival at his chambers, Mr. Beaumont lighted a cigarette, threw himself moodily into a big armchair, and proceeded to mentally review all his conduct towards Reginald since the lad's arrival in town.

Hard as he tried to find some flaw in his own conduct which might have put Blake on his guard, Beaumont was quite unsuccessful in doing so, for his demeanour towards his proposed victim had been all that the most delicate tactician could have desired.

"I can't have frightened him away, he said aloud to himself, "for I acted the disinterested friend to perfection. Hang it! I wonder what took him back to

Garsworth. I saw a letter in his hand, so I expect Una Challoner's been writing to him ; but that would not do me any harm, for she likes me, and I should think would be rather glad if I looked after the boy in town. I wonder if that confounded Patience has been talking ? I made things all straight before I left Garsworth, but one never knows what may happen, and if Patience got an inkling of my design, she'd move heaven and earth to get the boy back again to her side—humph ! I hardly know what to think—that's the worst of dealing with women ; they're so crooked, you never know what they're going to do next."

He arose from his seat and walked impatiently up and down the room, seeking some solution of the problem thus presented to him. While doing so, he happened to glance at the mantelpiece, and saw thereon a letter.

"I wish that man of mine wouldn't put the letters there," he grumbled, taking the letter, "I can never find them—but let me see who this is from ; Garsworth postmark—don't know the writing—wonder if Una Challoner is—by Jove!" he ejaculated, as he took out the letter and glanced at the signature, "it's from Patience Allerby. I knew she had been up to some mischief. Well, I'll read the letter, and see if I can't foil you, my lady."

Resuming his seat in the arm-chair, he smoothed out the letter carefully as he prepared to read it. The contents, which were as follows, considerably astonished him, and his lips curled with a cynical smile as he glanced down the closely-written page.

"BASIL BEAUMONT,—

"*Is it true what Dr. Nestley has told me—that you are in love with Una*

Challoner? If it is, I will make an end of everything between us, and denounce you, even at the cost of my own liberty. You have ruined my life, but you are not going to ruin that of my son by taking from him the woman he loves.

Reginald Blake is now in London, and I hear you are constantly by his side. Act honourably by him, or I swear I will punish you for any harm you do to him. By our mutual sin he is now in possession of the Garsworth estate, and is going to marry the lawful mistress of it. As this is the case, and his marriage to Miss Challoner is the one atonement both of us can make for depriving her of her inheritance, you must let things take their course. You have a desperate woman to deal with in me, and if you harm either Reginald or his promised wife in any way, I swear by all that I hold most sacred that you shall stand in the prisoner's dock for conspiracy, even though I have to stand by your side as an accomplice.

"PATIENCE ALLERBY."

Beaumont laughed sardonically as he finished this letter, and twirling it in his fingers, looked thoughtfully at the carpet.

"I wonder," he said at length, in a low voice, "I wonder if this letter means love of her son or jealousy of Una; both I expect, for though she hates me like poison, and everything sentimental between us is dead and buried years ago, she gets mad as soon as she thinks I admire another woman—strange thing a female heart— whatever ashes of dead loves may remain in it, there is always some live ember hidden beneath—humph! queer thing that the love of twenty years ago should suddenly spring up again to life."

He arose from his seat, and commenced once more to walk up and down the room,

soliloquising in a low voice, while outside
the fog was growing quite black and a
sombre twilight spread through the apart-
ment.

" So it's Nestley I've got to thank for
rousing her suspicions. He's been giving
Patience his view of my character, which
no doubt will coincide with her own—
amiable creatures both! She has told Una
that there is danger to Reginald in my
companionship, so either herself or Una
have written to town and frightened my
shy bird into taking flight. Bother these
women, how dreadfully they do upset one's
plans ; however, I do not mind, my hold
upon Reginald Blake is just as firm at
Garsworth as it is in London. As to
Patience denouncing me—pish !—melodramatic rubbish—it's too late now to talk
such nonsense—if she tells the truth her son
loses the property, and she's too fond of
him to risk that. As to Blake himself,

when he knows I'm his father he'll be glad enough to make terms or lose the property and Una Challoner."

He paused a moment, lighted a cigarette, and going to the window gazed absently out into the black mist which clung around the roofs and chimney-pots of the houses, and hid the brilliantly lighted street below from his gaze.

" Una Challoner," he murmured thoughtfully. "Patience thinks I'm in love with her. Curious that I am not; she has everything a woman can have to attract and allure a man, and yet I don't care a bit about her. Had I been in love with her I would not have troubled my head about Reginald, but let Una inherit the property, and then it would have been a tug of war between father and son as to who married the heiress! That I have secured the property for our son ought to easily convince Patience that I love money

more than Una Challoner, but of course
she doesn't see because she is blinded by
jealousy—rather complimentary to me I
must say, seeing how hard I tried to break
her heart in the past."

Turning away from the window with a
sigh he lighted the gas, then going over to
the mirror placed over the fireplace he
looked at himself long and critically.

" You're growing old, my friend," he
murmured, " the wine of life is running to
the lees with you, and I'm afraid you'll
never fall in love again—still it's wonderful
how I keep my good looks—my face is my
fortune—ah, bah ! and what fortune has it
brought me ? two dismal rooms, a pre-
carious existence, and not a friend in the
world."

He laughed drearily at the dismal pros-
pect he had conjured up and pursued his
meditation.

" I'll make one more bid for fortune, and

I think I hold strong cards. If I win—as I can't help doing—I'll turn over a new leaf and become respectable. But if I lose, and there are always the possibilities of losing, I'll throw up the sponge in England and try my luck in America. If I don't succeed there, perhaps a friendly cowboy will put an end to my wasted life; at present, *carpe diem*, as our friend the vicar would say, so I'll dine at the club and scribble a letter to Patience Allerby."

He dressed himself slowly, still in a dismal mood, and as he was rattling along in a hansom he gave himself an impatient shake.

" Bah," he muttered with a shiver, " I've got a fit of the blue devils with this weather. Never mind, a good dinner and a bottle of wine will soon put me right."

He had both, and felt so much better that he began to view things in a more

rosy light, and wrote a letter to Patience
Allerby which entirely satisfied him.

" There," he said gaily, as he dropped it
into the box, " I think that will show my
lady pretty plainly how I intend to proceed,
so now as there's nothing better to do I'll
go to the theatre."

And to the theatre he went, trying by
every means in his power to shake off by
means of this fictitious gaiety the gloomy
thoughts which always beset him when he
found himself alone.

CHAPTER IX.

THE CALM BEFORE THE STORM.

After great troubles our lives rearrange themselves in new forms, which last only until some later evil arises therefrom to alter them once more, and these latter in their turn are subject to further changes, so that from cradle to tomb our fortunes alter in divers ways every moment of our existence.

So the prodigal son had returned after his perilous wanderings in far lands, and his home circle killed the fatted calf and made merry in token of rejoicing. When Una saw how haggard the young man was in appearance and how depressed in mind, she felt deeply grateful to Providence that the chance words of Nestley had led her to write the letter which had induced her lover to return. Now that he was once more by her side she determined that

38*

nothing should ever part them again, and longed eagerly for the marriage to take place which should give her the right to go through life by his side. Doubtless many people would consider such longing hardly compatible with maiden modesty, but Una was too pure and sensible a woman to look at things in such a false light. She ardently loved Reginald and he returned that love, why then should she, for the sake of conventional appearance, risk her life's happiness by delay, seeing that everything was now at stake? No! she was determined to get married to Reginald as soon as possible, so that he would not be lured to destruction by evil counsel and wicked companions. It was not that she mistrusted her lover, for she well knew his straightforward, honourable nature, but it was better to leave nothing to chance, as even the strongest of men is not proof against temptation.

A week after Reginald arrived they were seated in Dr. Larcher's study talking over the question of the marriage, and the vicar was inclined to agree with their desire that it should be soon, although he was unwilling they should be blamed for undue haste.

" The world, my dear Una, is censorious," he said, wisely, " and as the Squire has only been dead two months it will be as well to wait a little longer."

" I suppose so," replied Una with a sigh, " although I do not see it would mean any disrespect to his memory if we got married at once."

" No doubt, no doubt—still *medio tutissimus ibis*, and I think it will be wiser for you both to put off the marriage for at least three months."

" Three months," said Reginald, with a groan, " that's as bad as three years, but I suppose we must—I will stay at Garsworth in the meantime."

" Of course, my dear boy, of course," answered the vicar, crossing his legs and placing his thumbs and forefingers together " you can take up your old life again."

" Ah, never ! never again," said the young man, shaking his head sadly, " the old life is dead and done with. I have eaten of the tree of knowledge, and the fruit is bitter."

" My dear Reginald," said Una, crossing over to him and putting her kind arms round his neck, " you must not be so despondent—it is not your fault."

" The sins of the father are visited on the children," he replied gloomily, " if it had been anything else I would not have minded—but to be what I am—a nobody —entitled to bear no name—it is bitter, very bitter indeed. I've no doubt I should be above such petty pride, still I am but mortal, and disgrace is hard to bear."

" If it is disgrace I will bear it with you," whispered Una, smoothing his hair, " we will be married and go away for a time ; you will soon forget the past when we go abroad."

" With your help I hope to," he said, looking affectionately into her clear eyes shining down on him with ineffable love in their azure depths.

" I think," remarked the vicar, touched by the deep sorrow of the young man, " that taking all things into consideration it would be wiser to do as you wish."

" And marry ? " cried Reginald eagerly.

" And marry," assented the vicar, nodding good-naturedly ; " what says Horace ? ' *carpe diem quam minimum credula postero.*' So taking that advice it will be best for you both to be married quietly next week and go abroad for a time—when you return Reginald will doubtless find his position easier."

" I hope so," said Blake, mournfully, as they arose to go, " but I'm afraid it's hopeless—this discovery has killed all the pleasures of life—my youth is dead."

" The soul is immortal," said Dr. Larcher solemnly, " and on the ruins of your joyous youth, which you regard as dead, you can raise the structure of a nobler and wiser life—it will be hard, but with Una to help you, not impossible — '*nil mortalibus arduum est.*' "

And they went away from the presence of the old man—he with resignation in his breast, and she with whispering words of comfort on her lips, infinite pity in her eyes, and enduring affection in her heart.

Patience Allerby was delighted when she heard how soon the marriage was to take place, as she dreaded lest through the machinations of Beaumont it should be broken off. Once Reginald was married to Una he would be safe both as regards fortune and position, for nothing Beaumont could reveal concerning the conspiracy would alter the state of affairs, and her one aim in life, to secure happiness for her son, would thus be accomplished.

At present, however, she dreaded every day either to see Beaumont or hear from him, especially after the warning letter she had written; nor was she disappointed, for a week after Reginald's return she received a letter from her quondam lover informing her that he was coming down in order to have a proper understanding with his son.

"*The young rascal has more firmness of purpose than I gave him credit for,*" he wrote in a cynical vein, "*and took less eagerly to the dissipations of London than I should have expected. I am afraid he inherits your cold blood, and not the hot temperament of his father, otherwise he would hardly have left the only city fit to live in for a dull hole like Garsworth. However, I see plainly he is a clod and lacks the divine zest necessary to enjoy life, so I suppose he has returned in perfect contentment to marry Una Challoner and live the bovine life of a country squire. So be it! I certainly do not mind, but first he must settle with me. I have placed him in a good position and given him a large income, so for these services I must be recompensed, and am coming down to have an interview with him on the subject. If he is wise, he will seek to know no more than he does, but if he inherits your obstinate nature and wants to know all, I am afraid he will have to learn the truth. Even then it will not be too late, for I will hold my tongue as to his real birth, and leave him in full possession of his wealth provided I am well paid for such silence. Now*

*that you understand the situation you had
better prepare him to receive me as one who
desires to be friendly—if he treats me as an
enemy he will find me a bitter one, so he had
better be sensible and come to terms. As to
my love for Una Challoner, you ought to know
by this time I love no one but*

" Yours truly,

" BASIL BEAUMONT."

This brutal letter fell like a lump of ice
on the heart of the unhappy Patience, as
she saw the net gradually closing round
her. She knew only too well that Beaumont would do what he said unless some
arrangement could be made—and then, as
Nestley said he loved Una, he would doubtless want to marry her as well as gain an
income, and their son would be left miserable. No, she would not have it, this devil
would not be permitted to sin any more
and ruin lives with impunity as he had

hitherto done. She made up her mind to see him before his interview with Reginald, and make one last appeal to his feelings as a father; if he refused to grant her prayers and keep the boy ignorant of his real birth she would reveal all herself and bear the shame sooner than he should tempt Reginald to a sin. When all was told, she would implore Una to still marry her son, and then depart to bury herself in solitude, and expiate her sins by years of repentance.

Events were still in the future, and she knew not how they would turn out, but of one thing she was determined, that Beaumont should not blight and ruin her son's life as he had blighted and ruined her own.

CHAPTER X.

A RUINED LIFE.

" Is this the end of all the years
　　That thou hast lived, my friend ?
Of merry smiles and bitter tears
　　Is this the end ?
Tho' sad and dark the past appears,
　　God to thy soul will courage send,
And Christ will whisper in thine ears
The word which hearts desponding cheers ;
　　So rise and to thy work attend,
Nor let the wicked ask with jeers
　　' Is this the end ? ' "

A FEW days after a decision had been arrived at concerning the marriage Basil Beaumont made his reappearance in Garsworth, and took up his old quarters at " The House of Good Living," in order to come to a final understanding with Reginald Blake.

The artist was in an excellent humour,

for, according to his own judgment, he was
master of the situation. He had only to
threaten Reginald with the loss of his newly
acquired wealth, and, judging the young
man's nature by his own, he felt satisfied
that, sooner than surrender Garsworth
Grange, the false heir would pay him a
handsome income to hold his tongue.
With such income he would retire to the
Continent and amuse himself for the rest of
his life; while, as for Patience, seeing that
he had no further use for her, she could
make what arrangement she liked with
Reginald, and please herself in her manner
of living. With all this astute calculation,
however, Beaumont made no allowance for
the different nature of his son, and did not
for a moment think that the young man's
nobility of soul would induce him rather to
resign everything, at whatever cost, than
keep possession of what he knew was not
rightfully his own.

He learnt from Kossiter that Reginald and Una were going to be married the next week, and smiled cynically to himself as he thought how easily he could stop the ceremony.

"If Una Challoner only knew the truth," he thought, "I think even her love would recoil from such a trial. Reginald Blake, the wealthy bastard, is one thing; but Reginald Blake, the pauper bastard, is another. Yes, I think I hold the best hand in this game; as to Patience! bah! my cards are somewhat too strong for her to beat."

Mr. Beaumont had only arrived a short time, and was seated before the fire smoking in the dull light of the winter afternoon, preparatory to writing a letter to Reginald. Margery, bright and alert, was clearing away the luncheon; so Mr. Beaumont, wishing to be quite sure of his ground, began to question her concerning the events which had taken place during his absence.

"I hear Miss Challoner is going to be married to Mr. Blake," he said genially; " it's a good match for her."

" And for him, too, sir," retorted Margery indignantly. "Miss Una is as sweet a young lady as you will find anywhere."

"No doubt," answered Beaumont blandly. " They are a charming couple, and certainly deserve the good opinion of everybody; but tell me, Margery, what about Dr. Nestley? I suppose he has gone long ago?"

" No," said Margery, shaking her head; " he is still here."

" In this place?"

" Yes, sir, very—very ill."

"Humph!" thought Beaumont, "got the jumps, I expect. What is the matter with him?" he asked aloud.

"He lost his way in the snowstorm last week," explained Margery deliberately, "and nearly died, but Farmer Sanders found him on the bridge and brought him here."

"Oh! and he is here still?"

"He is, sir. He was quite delirious, sir —raved awful. Dr. Blank's been attending him, and Miss Mosser."

"The blind organist—why has she turned nurse?"

Margery smiled in a mysterious manner.

"Well, folks say one thing and some folks say another," she replied, folding the table-cloth, "but I think she's in love with him; anyhow, as soon as she heard he was ill she came here like a mad woman, with Miss Busky, and both of 'em have been nursing him ever since."

"How good of them," said Beaumont ironically, "and is he better?"

"He's sensible," answered Margery cautiously, " but very weak. I don't know as he'll live."

" I'd like to see him. You know I'm a friend of his—do you think I could go up to his room ? "

" I don't know, sir," returned Margery stolidly. " I'll ask Miss Mosser."

" Do, that's a good girl," he replied, and Margery departed.

" Poor Nestley," muttered Beaumont to himself, lighting another cigarette, " it was rather a shame of me to have led him on like I did, but if I hadn't he would have interfered with my plans concerning old Garsworth, so I had to—self-preservation is the first law of nature. Come in," he called out, as a knock came to the door. " Come in, Margery."

It was not Margery, however, but Cecilia Mosser, who entered, with a pale sad face and a painfully-strained look in her sightless eyes.

"Mr. Beaumont," she said, in her low sweet voice.

"I am here, Miss Mosser," he replied, rising from his seat. "What can I do for you?"

"Nothing," she replied, groping her way to the table and standing beside it. "Are you alone?"

"Quite alone," returned Beaumont politely.

"You wish to see Dr. Nestley?"

"If I may be permitted."

"You will not be permitted," answered Cecilia slowly; "he is still very weak, and the sight of you would make him ill again."

"And why?" asked Beaumont, rather annoyed at the firmness of her tone; "surely a friend——"

"A friend," she interrupted, in a low vibrating tone. "Yes, a friend who is one in name only."

39*

"I don't understand you," said Basil politely. "What do you know of the friendship existing between myself and Dr. Nestley?"

"I know everything—yes everything—in his delirium he revealed more than he would have done——"

"Delirium—pshaw!"

"What he said then was confirmed by his own lips afterwards when he was sensible," she answered in a perfectly cool manner, "and I know how much your friendship has cost him—how you tried to drag him down to the lowest depths of iniquity. God knows for what end——"

Beaumont laughed in a sneering way, and leaned his shoulders comfortably against the mantelpiece.

"You seem to be in the confidence of our mutual friend," he said, in an easy tone. "May I ask why?"

"Because I am going to be his wife,"

replied Cecilia, while a flood of crimson rushed over the pure white of her face.

"His wife—a blind girl ? "

"Blind as I am he loves me," she said indignantly, "and I can protect him against you, Mr. Beaumont."

"Me ? I do not wish to harm him."

"No. You could not even if you did wish; he is going to marry me, and I hope to undo all the harm you have done him."

"I wish you joy of your task," he replied with a sneer. "But Dr. Nestley seems to be able to transfer his affections very easily —perhaps you do not know he was in love with Miss Challoner."

"Yes I do," she answered in a low tone, "he told me everything; and we under. stand one another perfectly. You have done your worst, Mr. Beaumont, and can do no more—he is going to become my husband, and, blind as I am, I hope to be his guardian angel from such men as you."

"These domestic details don't interest me in the slightest," he answered contemptuously, waving his hand. "Will you be kind enough to go, Miss Mosser? I have some letters to write."

"I am going," answered the blind girl, quietly feeling her way to the door. "I only came to tell you that you will never see him again—never!"

"Neither will you," he returned brutally.

The poor girl burst into tears at the unmanly taunt, but hastily dried them, and answered him back proudly.

"I can see him in my own mind, sir," she said indignantly, "and that is all I wish for—his faults have been of your making, and not of his own. I say good-bye to you, sir, and only wish you a better heart, that you may not make a jest of the misfortunes of others."

As she closed the door after her, Beaumont felt rather ashamed of himself, but soon recovered from the feeling, and sat down at the table to write a note to Reginald.

"Bah!" he said, as his pen travelled swiftly over the paper. "What do I care? if he likes to encumber himself with that woman he can do so. I don't suppose I'll ever see him again in this life, nor do I wish to—my business now is with my dear son. I'll get what I want out of him, and then the whole lot of them can go to the devil."

Meanwhile, Cecilia had returned to the sick room, where Miss Busky, still faithful to her blind friend, sat watching by the bed-side of the invalid. A pale, sickly light filtered in through the white-curtained windows, mixing with the red glow of the fire, and in this curiously blended twilight could be seen the glimmer of the medicine bottles on the round table by the bed, the deep arm-chair close at hand wherein Miss Busky sat, the milky whiteness of the dis-ordered bed-clothes and the subdued shine upon the surface of the furniture. Through-out the room was a complete stillness, unbroken even by the tick of a clock, and nothing was heard but the heavy breathing of the sick man.

As Cecilia entered, Miss Busky arose lightly to her feet and crossed over to her friend, speaking in a subdued whisper.

"Did you see him?" she asked.

"Yes—he will not come up, thank Heaven!—Dr. Nestley suspects nothing? '

"Nothing!—he is asleep—let me place you in the chair—I'm going out for a few minutes."

She led Cecilia forward, and the blind girl sank into the arm-chair; then, hastily putting on her hat, Miss Busky glided rapidly out of the room, leaving Cecilia seated by the bed, listening to the breathing of the invalid.

So still, so quiet — it might almost have been the silence of the tomb. Then there came the light patter of rain-drops on the windows. The fire had sunk to a dull red glow, and a piece of burning coal dropped, with a singularly distinct noise, on to the fender. Nestley sighed in his sleep—moved uneasily, and then awoke—a fact which the blind girl was aware of immediately, by her acute sense of hearing.

"Cecilia," said the sick man, in a weak voice.

"I am here, dear," she replied softly. "Do you want anything?"

He put out his hand and clasped one of hers in his feeble grasp.

"Only you—only you—I thought you had left me."

" Hush !—you must not speak much,"
she said, arranging the bed-clothes.

"I have had a dream," whispered the
invalid fearfully, "a strange dream— that
I was in the coils of a serpent, being
crushed to death.   But a woman suddenly
appeared, and at her touch the serpent
vanished and I was free.   The woman
had your face, Cecilia."

" Hush—do not speak more—you are
too weak—you are in safety now, and
no serpent shall touch you while I am
by your side."

" You will be my wife ? "

"I will be your wife," she replied
softly.   "I have loved you from the
first day I met you, but never thought
you would be burdened with such a useless thing as I."

" Not useless, dear.   How could I
have been so foolish as not to have
understood your love before ?   Thank

God for this illness, that has opened my eyes. You have saved my life — my soul."

He stopped, through exhaustion, and lay silently upon his pillow, watching the red flare of the fire glimmer on the pale face of the blind girl. A great feeling of joy and thankfulness came over him, as he felt that all the stormy, tempestuous life of the past was over at last—and beside him sat the one woman who could save his weak nature from yielding to the temptations of the world.

CHAPTER XI.

" Madonna, who hath ever stood
   As type of holy motherhood,
   I pray thee, for thy Son's dear sake,
   This sorrow from my bosom take.
   For there are those, with anger wild,
   Who wound the mother thro' the child.
   I know that thou wilt pity me,
   For thy Son hung upon the tree,
   And as He died to save and bless,
   Oh, help me, thou, in my distress."

AFTER he had finished a very nice little dinner, with a small bottle of champagne to add zest to it, Mr. Beaumont lighted a cigarette, and sat down comfortably before the fire, in order to wait for Reginald Blake. He had written to the young man, announcing his arrival and asking him to call, so he had no doubt but that he would be favoured with a visit. Having, therefore, arranged his plan of action, he lay back indolently in his chair, making plans for the future, and building air-castles amid the blue spirals of smoke which curled upward from his lips.

About seven o'clock he heard a knock at the door, and in answer to his invitation to enter, a woman made her appearance. Beaumont, who had merely turned his head to greet Reginald, was rather astonished at this unexpected guest, and arose to his feet in order to see who it was. His visitor closed the door carefully after her and stepped forward so that she came within the circle of light cast by the lamp on the table, then, throwing back her veil, looked steadily at the artist.

" Patience ! "

" Yes, Patience," she replied, sitting down on a chair near the table. " You did not expect to see me ? "

"Well, no," answered Beaumont, indolently leaning against the mantelpiece. "I must confess I did not—but if you want to speak with me, I can spare you very little time, as I am waiting——"

"For Reginald?" she interrupted quickly. "Yes, I know that."

"The deuce you do! What a wonderful woman you are! How did you find out I was here?"

"I left instructions that I was to be informed of your arrival, as I wished to speak with you before you saw our son."

"Indeed! And what do you want to speak to me about?"

"Your letter."

"I think my letter was too clear to require further explanation," he said impatiently. "I told you my intentions."

"You did—and I have come to tell you they will not be carried out."

"Is that so?" said Beaumont, with a sneer. "Well, we'll see. Who will prevent me doing what I like?"

"I will."

"Really—I'm afraid you over-rate your powers, my dear Patience. You are a clever woman, no doubt—a very clever woman—but there are limits."

"As you observe, very truly, there are limits," she retorted fiercely, "and those limits you have overstepped. Do you think I am going to stand by and see you wring money out of my son?"

"Our son," he corrected gently. "You forget I am his father. As to wringing money out of him, that's a very unpleasant way of putting it. I simply propose to appeal to his common sense."

"Sit down," said Patience, suddenly. "I wish to speak to you."

Beaumont shrugged his shoulders, then, pushing the arm-chair to one side, sat down in it so that he faced her fairly, keeping, however, with habitual caution, his face well in the shade,

"By all means," he said amiably. "I always humour a woman when there is nothing to be gained by doing otherwise. Go on, my dear friend, I'm all attention."

The housekeeper was leaning forward, resting her elbows on the table, and he could see her finely-cut, bloodless face— looking as if carved out of marble, in the yellow rays of the lamp-light—with her nostrils dilated, her lips firmly closed, and her black eyes sparkling with suppressed anger.

"I see it's going to be a duel to the death," he said, in a mocking tone, leaning his head against the cushion of the chair. "Well, I do not mind—I'm fond of duels."

"You are a fiend!" she burst out angrily.

"Really! Did you come all this way to impart that information? If so, you have wasted your time. I've heard the same remark so often."

His brutally cool manner had a wonderfully calming effect upon her, for after this one outburst of anger, she appeared to crush down her wrath by a strong effort of will, smiled disdainfully, and went on to speak in a cold, clear voice.

"Listen to me, Basil Beaumont: years ago you did me the worst harm a man could do a woman—you destroyed my life, but thanks to my own cleverness I managed to preserve at least the outward semblance of a pure woman without sacrificing our son in any way, but do you think that has cost me nothing—do you think I did not feel bitter pangs at having to deny my own son, and to veil my maternal longings under the guise of a servant? I did so, not so

much to preserve my own good name as to
benefit the boy.   I wanted him to think he
had no heritage of shame, so that he could
feel at least pride and self-respect.   When I
obtained the reward of my sacrifice—when
I saw that my son was satisfied with his lot
and had talents to make his way in the
world you came down for the second time
to ruin not my life, but his—the life of an
innocent being, who had never done you
any harm.   I entered into your vile conspiracy because I thought it would benefit
my son, and now I repent bitterly that I
ever did so. Owing to the foul lie you com-
pelled me to tell, he has gained a fortune,
but lost his self-respect. You do not understand the feeling, because your heart these
many years has been steeped in wickedness,
but think what it has done to our unhappy
child—cast a blight upon his life which no
money, no position can ever remove—his
youth died from the moment I told him

that lie, and whose work is it—mine or yours, Basil Beaumont? Mine or yours?"

She paused a moment, moistened her dry lips with her tongue, and then went on speaking rapidly with vehemence.

"And now when the worst is over—when he is firmly settled in possession of that wealth it has cost him his youthful happiness to gain—when he is going to marry the woman he loves, who will be able to comfort him in some measure—you once more return to work ruin for the third time —you demand money to hush up a disgraceful secret—you would not only tell him that he is still a nameless outcast, but you would take all his money from him, yes, and take also the girl who is to be his wife—you would leave him a pauper—an outcast—a miserable being with neither self-respect, nor riches, nor consolation. I implore you for my sake—for his sake—for your own sake, not to do this—our crime

40*

has shadowed his young life too much already—tell him no more—go away from this place, and let him have at least one chance of happiness."

She arose to her feet at the last words, and stretched out her arms appealingly towards Beaumont with humid eyes and an imploring expression on her face. The artist sat silent, smiling cynically, with a savage glitter in his eyes, and when she had finished, broke into a hard laugh as he also rose to his feet, flinging his cigarette viciously into the fire.

"A very pretty thing to ask me to do," he said mockingly, "and a very useless request to make. Do you think I care for his feelings or yours?—not the snap of a finger. I put Reginald in possession of the Garsworth estate not for his own sake, but for mine. Had he been wise and allowed me to guide him, he would have known no more than he does now. If he gives me the money I ask, it is even now not too late, but I am not going to spare him, either for his own sake or yours. He will be here soon, and I will tell him everything, so if he does not give me what I ask, I'll ruin him body and soul."

Patience flung herself at his feet, and burst into tears.

" For God's sake, Basil, spare him."

" No."

" He is your child."

" The more reason for him to help me."

" Have you no mercy ? "

" None—if it means getting no money."

" For my sake, spare him."

" For your sake least of all."

" You intend to tell him ? "

" I do. You can save yourself the trouble of making this melodramatic ex- hibition. I'm not going to move one hair's breadth from the position I have taken up. I want money, and I mean to have it."

Patience sprang to her feet in an access of mad fury and stood before him with clenched hands and blazing eyes.

"Are you not afraid I'll kill you?"

"Not a bit."

"You defy me."

"I do."

She drew a long breath, and snatched up her gloves from the table, her passion subsiding under his cool brutality as a stormy sea subsides when oil is cast upon the waters.

"Very well," she said coolly. "I'll tell everything to Doctor Larcher, and get him to prosecute both of us for conspiracy. I will stand in the dock and you beside me."

Beaumont laughed sneeringly.

"I've no doubt you will stand in the dock," he said with emphasis, "but not me. I have done nothing in the matter, you everything. Who is to prove I hypnotised the old man, and forged the papers making Reginald the heir?—no one. Who is to

prove that you falsely passed off your son
as the heir?—everyone.   You are the sole
representative of the conspiracy, and I shall
simply deny the whole affair.   It will be
my word against yours, and with such
strong evidence as can be brought against
you I fancy you'll get the worst of it."

An expression of terror passed over the
face of the unhappy woman as she saw
what a gulf was open at her feet.   It
was true what he said—she was the only
one who had spoken—to all outward
appearances he had in nowise been im-
plicated in the conspiracy.   With a cry of
despair, she reeled back against the wall,
covering her face with her hands... At that
moment Reginald's voice was heard outside,
and with a rapid movement, Beaumont
sprang forward and caught one of her wrists
in his grip.

" Here is Reginald," he said in a harsh
whisper, " hold your tongue or it will be

the worse for you.   I don't want him to see you—hide in here and keep silent.   What I intend to do will depend upon the result of this interview."

Patience said nothing, as all power of will seemed to have deserted her, but allowed herself to be dragged towards a door in the wall which communicated with a stair-case leading to the upper part of the house. Pushing her in here, Beaumont closed the door, then rapidly returned to the fire-place and flung himself into his chair.

" Act I. has been rather **stormy**," he said to himself with a sneer.   " I wonder what Act II. will be like."

CHAPTER XII.

FATHER AND SON.

Father !—art thou my father ?—pause, good sir,
Ere thou profanest thus that holy name.
A father should protect and guide his child
Through the harsh tumult of this noisy life,
But thou hast stood apart these many years
And left me to the mercy of the world,
With all its snares and madd'ning influence,
Yet now thou say'st " I am thy father "—nay,
No name is that for such a one as thou.

LOOKING at that quiet room illuminated by the mellow light of the lamp, no one could have imagined the scene of terror and despair which had lately taken place, yet when Reginald entered, his face wore a somewhat puzzled expression.

" How do you do, Beaumont ? " he said as the artist arose with a frank smile and took his hand. " I thought I heard a scream."

" Did you ? " replied Beaumont, assisting

his visitor to remove his great coat. "Then
I'm afraid I must have been asleep, as I
heard nothing, not even your knock; the
opening of the door aroused me."

"I didn't knock at all," said Reginald,
sitting down by the fire and drawing his
chair closer to the burning coals. "I
should have done so, but I forgot and
walked straight in—you don't mind, do
you?"

"Not at all, my boy, you are perfectly
welcome," answered the artist heartily.
"Will you smoke?"

"Thank you, I've got my pipe."

He lighted his pipe and lay back in the
chair watching the fire, while Beaumont,
bending forward with his face in the shadow
puffed at his cigarette, watching Reginald,
and crouching on the dark staircase with
her eye to the keyhole, a silent woman
watched both. It was a curious situation
and not without a touch of grim comedy,

though, as a matter of fact, the play which the trio were about to act had more in it of the tragic than the comic element.

Reginald, looking sad and weary, watched the fire for some moments, till Beaumont, feeling the silence oppressive, broke it with a laugh.

"How fearfully dull you are, Blake," he said gaily, "is anything wrong?"

Blake withdrew his sad eyes from the fire and looked at the speaker with a singular smile.

"Not what many people would call wrong," he said at length. "I have a large income, I am young, and I marry the girl I love next week."

"Well, as you can't call any of those blessings wrong, my friend, you ought to be perfectly happy."

"No doubt—but perfect happiness is given to no mortal."

"You are very young to moralize," said Beaumont with a faint sneer.

"Yes, it appears absurd, doesn't it, but I can't help it; ever since I discovered the real story of my birth a shadow seems to have fallen on my life."

"And why—who cares for the bar sinister now-a-days?"

"Not many people I suppose, but I do —I daresay I have been brought up in an old-fashioned manner, but I feel the loss of my good name keenly—wealth can gild shame, not hide it."

"Rubbish! you are morbidly sensitive on the subject."

"No doubt I am—as I said before it's the fault of my bringing up—but come," he continued in a livelier tone, "I did not call to inflict my dismal mood upon you, let us talk of other things."

"Such as your marriage?"

"Certainly—marriage is a pleasant sub-

ject," said the young man with a quiet
smile. " As I told you, I marry Miss
Challoner next week and then we go abroad
for a year or two."

" And what about your property in the
meantime ? " asked Beaumont.

" Oh, I'll leave it to my solicitors to
attend to."

" Why not appoint me your agent ? "

Blake coloured a little at this direct
request and smiled in an embarrassed
manner.

" Well, I hardly see how I can do that,"
he said frankly, " I've only known you
about three months, and besides, I have
perfect confidence in my solicitors to manage
the property, so, with all due respect to
you, Beaumont, I must decline to appoint
you my agent."

He spoke with some haughtiness, as he
was irritated at the cool way in which
Beaumont spoke, but that gentleman seemed

in nowise offended and smiled blandly as he answered :

"If then, you will not help me in that way, will you give me some money—say five hundred pounds ?"

"Certainly not!" retorted Blake hotly, pushing back his chair, "why should I do such a thing? As I said before, I have only known you three months—you were kind enough to introduce me to some friends of yours in Town, beyond this our friendship does not extend—I have yet to learn that gentlemen go about requesting sums of money from comparative strangers."

"You have yet to learn a good many things," said Beaumont coolly, irritated by the independent tone of the young man, "and one is that you must give me the money I ask."

Blake jumped to his feet in amazement at the peremptory tone of the artist and looked at him indignantly.

"Must!" he repeated angrily, "I don't understand the word—what right have you to speak to me in such a manner?—if you think you've got a fool to deal with you are very much mistaken—I decline to lend or give you a sixpence, and furthermore I also decline your acquaintance from this moment."

He snatched up his overcoat and put it on, but Beaumont, still cool and unruffled, sat smiling in his chair.

"Wait a moment," he said slowly, "you had better understand the situation before you leave this room."

Reginald Blake, who had turned his back on the artist, swung round with a dangerous expression in his dark eyes.

"I understand the situation perfectly, sir; you thought I was a young fool, who, having come into money, was simple enough to play the part of pigeon to your hawk."

Beaumont arose slowly from his chair at this insulting speech, and frowned ominously, while the woman hidden behind the door watched the pair in a cat-like manner, ready to intervene if she saw cause.

"You had better take care, my boy," said Beaumont deliberately. "I am your friend now, beware lest you make me your enemy."

"Do you think I care two straws for either your friendship or enmity?" replied Blake with supreme contempt, looking the artist up and down. "If so, you are mistaken—what can you do to harm me I should like to know?"

"Then you shall know—I can dispossess you of your wealth and leave you a pauper."

"Hardly—seeing I now know your true character and touch neither dice-box nor cards."

"It will require neither dice-box nor cards," replied Beaumont, wincing at this home thrust, "I can dispense with those aids—and I can reduce you to your former position of a pauper and stop your marriage."

"Indeed! Then do so."

Beaumont was stung to sudden fury by the young man's coolness, and lost his temper.

"You defy me!" he hissed, advancing towards Blake. "You dare to defy me, you pauper—you outcast—you bastard!"

"Liar!"

In another moment Reginald had his hand upon Beaumont's throat, his face convulsed with rage, when suddenly Patience sprang forth from her hiding-place.

"Stop! He is your father."

Blake's grip relaxed, and his arm fell by his side, while Beaumont, stagger-

ing back, fell into the armchair and
began mechanically to arrange his dis-
ordered necktie.

"My father!"

It was Reginald who spoke in a dull,
slow voice, with his face ghastly pale
and his eyes fixed upon the cowering
form of the woman before him.

"My father! Is this true?"

Patience tried to speak, but her tongue
could not form the words, so Beaumont,
with a devilish light in his eyes, answered
for her.

"Quite true. Your mother has told
you."

"My mother! You?"

The young man looked from one to
the other in a dazed manner, then, with
a gasping cry, staggered forward and
seized Patience by the arm.

"Do you hear what this man says?"
he said in a strained, unnatural voice.

"That he is my father — that you are my mother! Is it true—tell me—is it true?"

"It is true."

A look of horror overspread his face, and flinging her away from him, with a cry of anguish he fell against the wall with white face and outstretched arms.

"My God! it is true."

His mother looked apprehensively at him for a moment, then fell on her knees weeping bitterly.

"Spurn me—curse me—despise me!" she cried in a broken voice. "You have every right to do so. I am your unhappy mother and he is your father. I lied when I said Fanny Blake and the squire were your parents. I lied at your father's instigation in order to gain you a fortune. He designed the conspiracy—I carried it out."

"And I have been the dupe of both,"

41*

interrupted Reginald fiercely, stepping
forward with uplifted hand as if to
strike her. "I don't believe this—it is
a lie! You are my nurse."

"I am your mother."

The calm manner in which she made
this assertion left no room for doubt,
and Reginald Blake recoiled from that
kneeling figure as if it had been a snake.

"My mother!" he muttered convulsively.
"Great Heavens! my mother!"

Patience saw how he shrank from her,
and a great wave of despair swept over
her soul as she struggled forward on her
knees, flinging out her arms towards him
with a bitter cry.

"Oh, forgive me—forgive me!" she
wailed. "I did it for the best; I did,
indeed. I denied you were my child in
order to save your good name, and I
only swore the lie about Fanny Blake
in order to make you rich. Do not

shrink from me, my son, I implore you.
Think how I have suffered all these years
—how I have sacrificed my life for your
sake. Have pity, Reginald, as you hope
for mercy. Have mercy!"

Reginald Blake stood quiet for a
moment, then, controlling himself by a
powerful effort, raised her to her feet.
As he did so she looked timidly at his
face, but saw therein no pity, no tender-
ness; only the look of a man suffering
agony. He placed her in a chair and,
without looking at her, advanced towards
the table.

"Before I can believe this story," he
said in a hard voice, "I require some
proof of it. By the squire's will the
property was left to the person who pro-
duced a certain paper, written by him,
and a ring. They were both found in
his desk, directed to me. If I am not
the squire's son how did this happen?"

"I can explain that very easily," replied Beaumont, taking some papers out of his breast coat pocket. "When I came down here a few months ago, I heard of the squire's madness regarding his reincarnation, and by means of a hypnotic sleep I found out from his own lips that he intended to leave all his property to a fictitious son, who was to be himself in a new body. Being under my control in the hypnotic state, he showed me where the paper and ring were hidden. I took them from their hiding place and filled up the paper with your name and that of Fanny Blake. I then enclosed the ring and paper in an envelope which the squire had directed to you, resealed it, and, getting the keys of his desk, placed them therein, where they were found. You understand?"

"I understand; but why did the squire direct an envelope to me?"

"Because he wanted to help you, and wrote this letter and this cheque, which he enclosed in an envelope to be given to you by your mother. I used the envelope as I explained, and kept the letter and cheque by me. Here they are as a proof of the truth."

Reginald took up the papers the artist placed upon the table and glanced over them, then placed them in his pocket, and turning away took up his hat.

"Where are you going?" asked Beaumont, alarmed at his action.

"I am going to see Dr. Larcher and tell him all," answered his son sternly. "What other course is there for me to take?"

"To hold your tongue," said the artist eagerly. "Surely you're not such a fool as to give up possession of an estate like this for a mere feeling of honour. Pay me a stated income and I will hold my

tongue.   Your mother will be silent for
her own sake, so no one will know the
truth."

Reginald looked at him with unutterable
contempt.

"After bringing me so low as you have
done do you think I am going to sink
lower of my own free will?" he said in a
scornful tone.   "No! a thousand times no.
I would not keep this property another
day if it were ten million a year.   I see
what your plan has been—to threaten me
with exposure if I did not bribe you to
silence.   You have mistaken me.   I am
not so base as that.   This property shall go
back to its rightful owner, and you will
not receive one penny either from her or
from me."

"I am your father."

"You are my father—yes, God help me!
If I am to believe this story you are my
father—a father I despise and loathe.   One

question more I only ask — are you my
mother's husband?"

" No," said Beaumont sullenly, " I am
not."

Reginald turned a shade paler and
laughed bitterly.

" What have I done to be punished like
this?" he said, raising his face in agony.
" You have taken away the wealth I
wrongfully possessed, you have deprived
me of my good name, of my self-respect,
but, as God is above us, you shall not
make me vile in my own sight by doing
your wicked will."

Another moment and the door closed, so
that Patience and Beaumont were alone.
Rising from her seat she took off her
bonnet.

" What are you going to do?" asked
Beaumont savagely, all his innate brutality
showing itself now that the mask was
dropped.

" I am going to stay here, to-night," she said, unsteadily walking to the door, " and to-morrow I will go to London, never to return."

" What about the Grange ? "

" I shall never go back to the Grange," answered the woman slowly, " there is no home for me there ; you have done your worst, Basil Beaumont—done your worst— and failed."

Again the door closed and Beaumont was left alone—alone with his ruined hopes and his despair.

" Failed," he muttered savagely, looking into the fire. " Yes, I have failed to get the money, but I shall not fail to ruin Reginald Blake for all that ; he thinks he will still marry the heiress of the Grange ; he can set his mind at rest—he will never marry Una Challoner."

CHAPTER XIII.

BEAUMONT PLAYS HIS LAST CARD.

Though he seems to thee an angel
    Let him not thy heart beguile,
He's a devil from a strange hell,
    Evil lurks beneath his smile.

ROUND the old Grange the winds were
howling dismally, and now that the thaw
had set in, the sadness of the place was
increased by the incessant dripping of the
melted snow. The dead leaves in the park
were sodden and heavy, so heavy, indeed,
that they could not be moved by the keen
wind, which, in revenge, shook the bare
boughs of the trees, or whistled dismally
through the cracks and crannies of the old
building.

Una sat at the window of the parlour
looking out at the heavy, grey sky, to

which the bleak trees lifted up their gaunt
arms, and listening to the monotonous
dripping on the terrace. But, in spite of
the dreariness and solitude of the place,
surely her heart should have been lighter
and her face gayer than it was, seeing that
in a few days she was going to be united to
the man she loved. But the shadow on
the dismal landscape also rested upon her
face, and even the lively chatter of Miss
Cassy about the wedding could not bring a
smile into her mournful eyes.

" I'm sure, Una, dear, I'm glad you're
going to be married," said Miss Cassy, who
had put the tea cosy on her head preparatory to leaving the room, " but really
I don't know what's coming over things ;
you look so sad—quite like a mourner, you
know—the Mourning Bride of what's-his-
name—and then for Patience to stay away
all night ! Why does she do it ?—why !—
why !—she never did it before, and then

those letters you got this morning, what
are they about ?—it's all so odd, I really
don't know what things are coming to."

"Things are going very well, aunt," said
Una with a faint smile. "Patience stayed all
night in the village because of the storm last
night, and as to those letters, I'll tell you
all about them later on."

"Yes, do, let me share your confidence,
at least. I brought you up from pinafores,
you know, quite like my own child. Oh,
I wish I had one. Why haven't I a child?
Now, I know what you're going to say—
marriage, of course—but I've never had the
chance, nobody wanted to marry me—so
odd—I would have made a loving wife—
quite like an ivy—really a clinging ivy.
Oh, if I could only find my oak."

The little lady fluttered tearfully out of
the room, leaving Una sitting alone with
the letters on her lap, looking out at the
dreary scene. She sighed sadly, and

gathering the letters together arose from her chair, when just at that moment a ring came to the front-door bell. Una started apprehensively and her pale face grew yet paler, but she said nothing, only stood like a statue by the window with an expectant look upon her face. Hardly had the harsh jingle of the bell ceased to echo through the house when Jellicks entered, and wriggling up to Una, announced in a hissing whisper that Mr. Beaumont desired to see her.

"Mr. Beaumont," murmured Una, starting suddenly, "what does he want, I wonder? I'd better see him, it may do some good—some good. Yes!" she said aloud, "I will see him; Jellicks, show Mr. Beaumont into this room."

She resumed her seat by the window as Jellicks vanished, and shortly afterwards the door opened and Basil Beaumont, looking haggard and fierce, stood before her.

He bowed, but did not attempt any warmer greeting, and she, on her part, simply pointed to a chair near her, upon which he took his seat.

"I suppose you are astonished to see me, Miss Challoner?" he said, after a pause.

"I confess I am a little," she replied calmly, "I thought you were up in London."

"So I was, but I came down to Garsworth yesterday."

"Indeed? Our quiet little village must have great attractions to draw you away from London."

"I did not come down without an object, Miss Challoner," he said gravely, "I have a duty to fulfil."

"Towards whom?"

"Yourself. Yes, I came down from London especially to see you."

"It's very kind of you to take so much trouble upon my account," she said coldly, looking keenly at him. "May I ask what this duty is to which you allude?"

"It is the duty of an honest man towards a wronged woman," said Beaumont quietly.

"Meaning me?"

"Meaning yourself," he asserted solemnly.

"You speak in riddles, Mr. Beaumont," said Una, folding her hands. "I will be very glad if you will explain them."

"Certainly. Two months ago your cousin died and left all his property to a supposed son, who turned out to be Reginald Blake ; I have now to inform you that Reginald Blake is no connection whatever of Squire Garsworth, consequently his assumption of the property is a fraud."

"What do you mean, sir?" said Una quickly. "I understood Mr. Blake's identity was fully established——"

"Yes, by Patience Allerby," interrupted Beaumont quickly. "She said he was the son of Fanny Blake and the Squire, knowing such a statement to be false."

" Then who are Mr. Blake's parents?"

" Patience Allerby and myself."

Una arose from her seat with an angry colour in her cheeks.

" You — you Reginald's father — impossible !"

" It's perfectly true," he replied calmly. " Patience Allerby came up to London many years ago with me, and when Reginald was born she left me and came down here, bringing up our son under another name. I, as you know, came to Garsworth some time ago, and saw her again, but she asked me to say nothing, so I obeyed her, but now that I find she has committed a fraud, of which you are the victim, I naturally hasten to put it right."

" Did Mr. Blake know he was not the heir ?"

" He did from the first," asserted Beau-

mont audaciously. "I have no doubt his
mother told him his true birth, and knowing the Squire's mania about re-incarnation
they made this conspiracy up together in
order to defraud you of the property."

"So Mr. Blake has deceived me?" said
Una, in an unnaturally quiet tone.

"Yes, he has deceived you all along. I
have no doubt he prepared all the forged
documents which proved his identity with
the supposed son, and counted on your love
for him not to prosecute should anything
be discovered. I'm glad I have been able
to warn you in time. You will never marry
him now."

"But the property; do you think he
will keep the property?"

"He will try to I've no doubt," said
Beaumont gravely, "but if you intrust
your case to experienced hands, I have no
doubt he will be made to disgorge his
plunder."

"But to whom can I turn?" said Una helplessly. "I have no friend."

Beaumont arose to his feet, and came close to her.

"Yes, you have one—myself."

"You?" she cried, recoiling with a shudder.

"Yes, I love you passionately, Una, and if you will by my wife, I will recover your property for you."

"But—your own son?"

"I despise a son who could act as Reginald has done. I came down here expecting to find an honourable man, but instead I discover a scoundrel, a forger, and a thief."

"Is it all true what you have said?" murmured Una, looking straight at him.

"All true," he answered solemnly, "I swear it."

"You liar!"

He started back in amazement, for she

42*

was facing him like an enraged tigress, with crimson cheeks and blazing eyes.

"What do you mean?" he said in a hoarse whisper.

"Mean?" she repeated scornfully. "That I know all, Basil Beaumont. Do you see this letter? I received it from your unhappy son this morning, giving me back the property and revealing the whole of your nefarious scheme. I know who forged the documents—you! I know who hoped to enjoy the money through Reginald —you! I know who comes with lies on his lips to part me from the only man I love—you! Yes—you! you! you!"

The baffled schemer stood nervously fingering his hat, with a white, sullen face, all his courage having left him. So mean, so cowardly, so despicable he looked, shrinking back against the wall before this young girl, who towered over him like an inspired Pythoness.

"You tell me Reginald Blake knew of this base conspiracy," she said with contempt. "Does this letter look like it? You say he will refuse to give up the property—this letter says he surrenders it of his own free will—and you have the insolence to speak of love to me. You—who so shamefully tricked and betrayed Patience Allerby — you contemptible hound!"

He tried to smile defiantly, and made an effort to form a word with his white, quivering lips, but both attempts were a failure, and without glancing at her he slunk towards the door, looking like a beaten hound.

"Yes, slink away like the craven you are," she cried disdainfully, "and leave Garsworth at once, or I will prosecute you for your scoundrelly conduct. Yes, though you were twenty times Reginald's father."

"I've spoilt his chance anyhow," he hissed venomously.

"You have spoilt nothing of the sort," she retorted superbly. "Do you think I believe the words of a vile thing like you against this letter? I am going to Reginald Blake to-day, and will place myself and my fortune in his hands—in spite of your falsehoods I will marry him, and he will still be master of Garsworth Grange—but, as for you, leave the village at once, or I will have you hounded out of it, as you deserve to be—you cur!"

White with anger and shame, he tried to speak, but with an imperious gesture she stopped him with one word:

"Go!"

He slunk out of the door at once, a ruined and disgraced man.

CHAPTER XIV.

A WOMAN'S HEART.

When Dame Fortune frowns severest,
  Then I love thee best of all,
I will cling to thee, my dearest,
  Though the world in ruins fall.

DR. LARCHER was in his study talking to
Reginald Blake, who sat near the writing
table, leaning his head upon his hand, with
his arm resting on the desk. The face of
the good Vicar was somewhat clouded, as
he felt deeply for the unhappy young man,
and he was trying to speak words of comfort to him, although he felt how difficult
it was to converse cheerfully under present
circumstances. Reginald, however, had
taken this second discovery more easily
than he had done the first, perhaps because
he had suffered so much already that he
could not suffer more. At all events, his

face, though pale, was perfectly composed, and there was a look of determination about his lips and a serene light in his eyes which gave great satisfaction to Dr. Larcher.

"I must say, my dear boy," he said kindly, "that you have great cause for sorrow, but you must bear adversity like a man, and I feel sure the result will be beneficial to your future life—sooner or later we all feel what Goëthe calls ' world sorrow,' and it is that which changes us from careless youth to thoughtful manhood —your trial has come earlier and has been a more bitter one than that of most men, but, believe me, out of this apparent evil good will come ; remember the saying of the old Roman lyrist, *Perrupit Acheronta Herculeus labor*—time will bring you relief, and, if you resist manfully, you also will be able to break through this Acheron of sorrow and pain."

Reginald listened attentively to this long discourse, and, at its conclusion, lifted his head proudly.

"I agree with all you say, sir," he replied steadily, "and hope to profit by your advice, but you must not think me a mere weakling who gives in without a struggle when trials come. No, I think your training has taught me more than that. I feel bitterly the circumstances of my birth, and in having parents I can neither honour nor respect ; but the cruellest blow of all is that I must renounce all hope of the woman I love—it is very hard, indeed, to almost gain the prize and then lose it through no fault of my own."

"I think you misjudge Una," said the vicar quietly, "she is not the woman to act in such a way—in fact, now that you have met with misfortune, I think she will love you more than before."

"I hope so, yet I doubt it," replied the

young man gloomily; " but now that all
my past is ended in ruin I must look to the
future and try and win a respected name,
which I have not got now.   But first, what
am I to do about my parents ? "

" Regarding your father," said the vicar
thoughtfully, "I don't think you will see
any more of him, as he will probably leave
the village to-day—now that he can gain
nothing from you he will doubtless leave
you alone—but as to your mother, your
place is certainly by her side."

" But   look   how   she   has   deceived
me."

"If she has erred it is through love of
you," replied Dr. Larcher gravely, " and
after all she is bound to you by the ties of
nature.   Yes, you must look after her ; but
what about yourself ? "

" I will go to London and make a fortune
by my voice."

" Your last sojourn in London was not

productive of any good result," said the vicar in gentle rebuke.

"Perhaps not, but if I erred it was with my head not my heart. I was miserable, and tried to drown my sorrows in dissipation; but now I go to town under widely different circumstances—a pauper where I once was wealthy—so my only dissipation now will be hard work."

"That is right," said the vicar, approvingly. "I am glad to see you accept the inevitable in such spirit—*levius fit patientia Quidquid corrigere est nefas.*"

"It's the only spirit in which I can accept the future," answered Reginald sadly, "seeing that I am to pass the rest of my life without Una."

"As I said before, you wrong her; she is too noble a woman to leave you now you are in trouble."

"I wish I was as certain as you are," said Blake, rising to his feet and walking to and fro, " but after what has passed I am afraid to hope."

At this moment a knock came to the door, and immediately afterwards Una Challoner entered. She looked pale in her dark mourning garments, but there was a soft light in her eyes as they rested on Reginald which comforted the vicar greatly.

"Welcome, my dear," he said heartily, rising and taking her hand, "you could not have come at a happier time. Reginald has great need of you, so I will leave you both together, and I hope you will prove the David to his Saul, in order to chase away the evil shadow that is on him."

When the vicar had departed and closed the door after him Una stood in silence, looking at Reginald, who had sat down again. So sad, so despondent was his attitude, that all the love of her heart went out towards him, and walking gently up to her lover she touched his shoulder.

"Reginald."

"Yes," he said, lifting his heavy eyes to her face. "What is it? Have you come to reproach me?"

"Reproach you with what, my poor boy?" she asked, tenderly, kneeling beside him. "What have you done that I should come to you with harsh words?"

"You are a good woman, Una," said Blake sadly, putting his hand caressingly upon her head, "but I think there is a limit even to your forbearance."

"What nonsense you talk," she said lightly. "I understand everything—you are not responsible for the sins of your parents."

"I cannot marry you now," he replied in a low voice. "I can offer you nothing except poverty and a dishonoured name."

"You can offer me yourself," said Una

with a smile, " and that is all I want.   As
to your dishonoured name, you forget you
have given that up—your name now is
Reginald Garsworth."

" It was, but I surrender it with the
property."

" I hardly see that, seeing there is no
question of surrender.   Yes," she went on,
seeing the astonishment depicted on his
face, " things are going to remain exactly
as they are.   You will still be titular lord
of the manor, and we will look upon this
conspiracy of your unhappy parents as if it
had never existed."

" Impossible," he muttered.   " I cannot
rob you of your property."

" Don't I tell you there is no robbery ? "
she replied rapidly.   " As man and wife
we will share the property in common, so
there is no necessity for you to surrender
what will soon come back to you by
marriage."

"I had given up all hope of the marriage!"

"Ah! you don't know how determined I am when I take a thing into my head," she said playfully. "We will be married next week, and you will retain the property just as if nothing had occurred. No one knows the truth of the affair except your parents, and they will not speak."

"My father will, I know his vindictive nature."

"Your father!" she repeated contemptuously. "Don't speak of Basil Beaumont by that name. He has been no father to you, and as for speaking you can set your mind at rest. He called upon me this morning, and I soon settled everything."

"He called on you?"

"Yes, with a lot of lies in his mouth, but I threatened to prosecute him if he did not leave the village, so by this time I think he is out of the neighbourhood. Don't trouble, my dear, Beaumont will hold his tongue for his own sake."

"And my mother?"

"I called at Kossiter's as I passed," she answered, "and found your mother had gone up to London this morning. We must find her out and give her some money to live on, for after all, whatever part she has taken in this conspiracy it was for love of you."

"Just what Dr. Larcher said."

"So you see everything is settled," she said joyously, rising from her knees, "we will be married next week and you will be master of Garsworth Grange."

Reginald was deeply affected by her noble conduct, and rising to his feet embraced her fondly.

"You are a noble woman," he said, with tears in his eyes, "but can I accept this sacrifice?"

"Why will you use such a word?—there

is no sacrifice in what I do for the man I love."

" Remember I bring you nothing.

"You bring me yourself, that is all I want. Let the past be forgotten. When we are married you will forget all the troubles you have had.

He kissed her, smiling.

"You are my good angel," he said simply.

CHAPTER XV.

THE DAWN OF A NEW LIFE.

On mount and mere the moonlight lies
Dim shadows veil the western skies,
On every stream the starlight gleams,
And all is mystery and dreams.
But now Night folds her sombre wings,
The lark his morning carol sings,
A rosy light glows o'er the lawn,
And lo ! in splendour breaks the dawn.

It was about a year since the marriage of
Una with Reginald, and they were standing
on the terrace of their hotel at Salerno,
which overlooked the sea. Far below lay
the blue ocean with its fringe of white
waves breaking on a shore that extended
in a curve round the base of the lofty
mountains, the summits of which were
clearly defined against the opaline sky.
And what a wonderful sky it was, for the
setting sun had irradiated the pure ether

with most gorgeous colours. Great golden clouds in the west, forming a canopy over the intolerable brilliance of the sinking sun, melted into a delicate rose colour, which, rising towards the zenith, imperceptibly dissolved into a cold, clear blue, out of which peered a few stars. There were some boats on the sea with their broad sails, and the young couple on the terrace could hear every now and then the shrill voice of a minstrel singing a popular Italian air to the clear notes of the mandolin.

It was a wonderfully picturesque scene, and one which would have enchanted the eye of an artist, but Mr. and Mrs. Garsworth, leaning over the terrace, were not looking at the splendours of sea and sky, being engaged, one in reading and the other in listening to a letter which appeared to interest them deeply.

They had been wandering about the Continent in a desultory kind of fashion

43*

for many months, exploring all kinds of old-fashioned cities, with their treasures of bygone ages. They had gazed at the splendours of the Alhambra at Granada, enjoyed the brilliant glitter of Parisian life, wandered in quiet Swiss valleys under the white crest of Mont Blanc, seen the Wagner Festival at Bayreuth, and dreamed of mediæval ages in the narrow streets of Nuremberg and Frankfort. Then coming south they had beheld with delighted eyes the white miracle of Milan Cathedral, passed enchanted moonlit hours in the palace-sided canals of Venice, idled amid the awesome ruins of the Eternal City, and after seeing the smoking crest of Vesuvius rise over the marvellous bay of Naples, had come to pass a few days at Salerno, that wonderfully picturesque town, which recalls to the student of Longfellow memories of Elsie and her princely lover.

Reginald was perfectly happy. He had,

it is true, lost all the gay carelessness of
youth, but in its place he had found the
deeper joy which arises out of a great
sorrow. There never was a more devoted
wife than Una, nor a more attached husband
than Reginald, and the bitter sorrow which
had shown them both how truly they loved
one another had borne good fruit, for they
had learnt to trust, love, and honour each
other so implicitly that no shadow ever
arose between them to darken their married
life. At Salerno, however, they had found
a letter from Miss Cassy, who had been left
in charge of Garsworth Grange, giving all
the news and urging them to return home
again. Nor was the request unwelcome,
for, now that his heart wound was to a
certain extent cured, Reginald began to tire
of the glowing landscapes of southern
Europe, and to long for that cold northern
land so fresh and green under its mists and
rain.

Una was reading the letter and Reginald, leaning his arms on the balustrade of the balcony, gazed idly at the fantastic splendours of the scene before him, listening eagerly to the news which brought so vividly before him the long marshes, the dreary Grange, and the quiet village life of Garsworth.

"I do wish you would come back, Una," wrote Miss Cassy, who, by the way, wrote exactly as she spoke, "it seems so odd the long time you've been away. According to your instructions the Grange has been done up beautifully, and I'm sure you will see how my taste has improved it. It's not a bit dreary now, but bright and homelike, and I'm sure you and dear Reginald will love it when you see it again. I do so long to hear about your travels—Rome and Santa Lucia, you know—it's a song, isn't it——?"

Curiously enough, as Una was reading
this the unseen minstrel below broke
into the well-known air with its charming refrain.   Reginald and Una looked
at one another and laughed.

"What a wonderful coincidence," said
Reginald, peering over the balcony to
see the musician; "if we told that to
Miss Cassy she wouldn't believe it; but
never mind, go on with the letter."

"I received a letter from Dr. Nestley,
the other day," read Una.   "Of course,
you know he married Cecilia Mosser, and
went home to his own place, at some
town in the North — I forget its name.
He is quite reformed now, and makes an
excellent husband.   I hear he is making
a good deal of money, and Cecilia is
organist at a church up there.   You
remember how beautifully she played?"

"I'm glad they are happy," interrupted Reginald, heartily.   "Poor Nestley's

life was nearly ruined by that scampish father of mine."

"I see Aunty says something about him," said Una, quickly. "She writes: 'In the letter I received from Dr. Nestley, he says he heard that Mr. Beaumont—you remember, Una?—who stayed at Garsworth—a charming man—is in America, and has married a very rich lady.'"

"I wish her joy of the bargain," said Reginald, grimly. "I suppose he has quite forgotten my poor mother."

"Never mind, dear," answered Una. "I'm sure your mother is much happier now."

"As a Sister of Mercy," said Reginald, in a musing tone, "poking about among the slums of London. It's a curious life for her to take up."

"I think she always had a leaning that way," replied Una with a sigh; "and it will make her forget the past."

"I wish she would accept some money, to make her comfortable."

"I don't think she will," said Mrs. Garsworth, folding up the letter; "but when we go back again, perhaps she'll give up London, and come back to Garsworth."

"I'm afraid not," replied Reginald, gravely. "My mother is a woman of strong will, and she thinks she has a sin to expiate, so she'll stay and labour there till she dies. Well, what else does Miss Cassy say?"

"Nothing particular," answered Una, putting the letter in her pocket. "Mrs. Larcher still labours under 'The Affliction.' Dr. Larcher has been to London, to attend some archæological meeting. Dick Pemberton has come in for his money, and, Aunty thinks, has some idea of asking Pumpkin to be his wife."

"Pumpkin?" echoed Reginald, in a shocked tone. "No, Una, you forget— Eleanora Gwendoline."

They both laughed, and Una went on giving the news.

"Jellicks and Munks are both well, and Ferdinand Priggs is going to bring out a new volume of poems."

"Is he, really?" said Reginald, lightly. "Don't I pity the unhappy public! But all this news makes me home-sick, Una."

"I feel exactly the same," she replied, rising to her feet, and slipping her arm into that of her husband. "Let us go home again."

"Yes, I think we will," said Reginald, after a pause. "I don't mind living at Garsworth, now you are with me, Una."

"And what about your voice?" she said, playfully. "Your wonderful voice, that was going to make your fortune?"

"Ah, that is a dream of the past,"

he said, half sadly. "I will settle down into a regular country squire, Una, and the only use I'll make of my voice will be to sing Lady Bell to you."

Then, putting his arm round her, he sang the last verse of the quaint old ballad:

"My Lady Bell, in gold brocade,
    Looked not so fair and sweet a maid,
    As when, in linsey woollen gown,
    She left for love the noisy town."

His voice sounded rich and full in the mellow twilight, while the minstrel below stopped playing, as he heard the song floating through the shadowy air. The sun had sunk into the sea, and the stars were shining brilliantly. One long bar of vivid light stretched along the verge of the horizon, and the air was full of shadows and the perfume of un-seen flowers.

"See!" said Reginald, pointing towards the band of light, "it is like the dawn."

"Yes!—the dawn of a new life for you and for me, dear," she whispered; and then they wandered along the terrace, through the shadows, with the hoarse murmur of the distant sea in their ears, but in their hearts the new-born feelings of joy and contentment.

THE END.

31, Southampton Street, Strand,
London, W.C.

WHITE & CO.'S

LIST OF

PUBLICATIONS.

New Novels at all Circulating Libraries.

THE MAN WITH A SECRET. By FERGUS HUME,
Author of "The Mystery of a Hansom Cab," &c. 3 vols.

THE MYSTERY OF M. FELIX. By B. L. FARJEON,
Author of "A Young Girl's Life," &c. 3 vols.

CRISS CROSS LOVERS. By the Honble. Mrs. H. W
CHETWYND. 3 vols.

A DAUGHTER'S SACRIFICE. By F. C. PHILIPS,
Author of "As in a Looking Glass," and PERCY FENDALL,
Author of "Spiders and Flies," &c. 2 vols.

A NEW OTHELLO. By IZA DUFFUS HARDY. 3 Vols.

BLINDFOLD. By FLORENCE MARRYAT, Author of
"My Sister the Actress" (2s.), "Facing the Footlights"
(2s. 6d.), &c. 3 vols.

TWO FALSE MOVES. By JEAN MIDDLEMASS. 3 Vols.

FAIRFAX OF FUYSTON; or a Practice Confess'd.
By MRS. HIBBERT WARE. 3 vols.

THE LAST OF THE CORNETS. By Col. ROWAN
HAMILTON. 2 vols. 12s.

ON THE CHILDREN. By ANNIE THOMAS (Mrs.
Pender Cudlip), Author of "Eyre of Blendon." 3 vols.

AN UNRULY SPIRIT. By Mrs. AYLMER GOWING,
Author of "The Jewel Reputation," &c. 3 vols.

FOR SOMEBODY'S SAKE. By EDITH STEWART
DREWRY 3 vols.

A CRUEL WRONG. By Mrs. HOUSTOUN, Author of
"Recommended to Mercy," "Barbara's Warning" (2s. 6d.),
&c. 3 vols.

THE M. F. H.'s DAUGHTER. By Mrs. ROBERT
JOCELYN, Author of "£100,000 versus Ghosts" (2 vols.), "A
Distracting Guest" (2 vols.), &c. 3 vols.

CASTE AND CREED. By Mrs. F. PENNY. 2 vols.

AN UNWILLING EXILE. By M. ANDRÉ RAFFALO-
VICH. 2 vols., 12s.

THE LOVE OF A LADY. By ANNIE THOMAS.
3 vols. (In August.)

THE NEW DUCHESS. By Mrs. ALEXANDER FRASER,
3 vols. (In August.)

F. V. WHITE & CO., 31, Southampton Street, Strand.

THE WORKS OF JOHN STRANGE WINTER.

UNIFORM IN STYLE AND PRICE.

Each in Paper Cover, 1/-; Cloth, 1/6.   At all Booksellers & Bookstalls.

FERRERS COURT.

BUTTONS.   (5th Edition.)

A LITTLE FOOL.   (6th Edition.)

MY POOR DICK.
(6th Edition.) Illustrated by MAURICE GREIFFENHAGEN.

BOOTLES' CHILDREN.
(7th Edition.) Illustrated by J. BERNARD PARTRIDGE.

"John Strange Winter is never more thoroughly at home than when delineating the characters of children, and everyone will be delighted with the dignified Madge and the quaint Pearl. The book is mainly occupied with the love affairs of Terry (the soldier servant who appears in many of the preceding books), but the children buzz in and out of its pages much as they would come in and out of a room in real life, pervading and brightening the house in which they dwell."—*Leicester Daily Post.*

THE CONFESSIONS OF A PUBLISHER.

"The much discussed question of the relations between a publisher and his clients furnishes Mr. John Strange Winter with material for one of the brightest tales of the season. Abel Drinkwater's autobiography is written from a humorous point of view; yet here, as elsewhere, 'many a true word is spoken in jest,' and in the conversations of the publisher and his too ingenuous son facts come to light that are worthy of the attention of aspirants to literary fame."—*Morning Post.*

MIGNON'S HUSBAND.   (9th Edition.)

"It is a capital love story, full of high spirits, and written in a dashing style that will charm the most melancholy of readers into hearty enjoyment of its fun."—*Scotsman.*

THAT IMP.   (9th Edition.)

"Barrack life is abandoned for the nonce, and the author of 'Bootles' Baby' introduces readers to a country home replete with every comfort, and containing men and women whose acquaintanceship we can only regret can never blossom into friendship."—*Whitehall Review.*

"This charming little book is bright and breezy, and has the ring of supreme truth about it."—*Vanity Fair.*

MIGNON'S SECRET.   (13th Edition.)

"In 'Mignon's Secret' Mr. Winter has supplied a continuation to the never-to-be-forgotten 'Bootles' Baby.' . . . The story is gracefully and touchingly told."—*John Bull.*

F. V. WHITE & Co., 31, Southampton Street, Strand.

THE WORKS OF JOHN STRANGE WINTER—*(continued)*.

ON MARCH. (7th Edition.)

"This short story is characterised by Mr. Winter's customary truth in detail humour, and pathos."—*Academy.*

"By publishing 'On March,' Mr J. S. Winter has added another little gem to his well-known store of regimental sketches. The story is written with humour and a deal of feeling."—*Army & Navy Gazette.*

IN QUARTERS. (8th Edition.)

"'In Quarters' is one of those rattling tales of soldiers' life which the public have learned to thoroughly appreciate."—*The Graphic.*

"The author of 'Bootles' Baby' gives us here another story of military life, which few have better described."—*British Quarterly Review.*

ARMY SOCIETY; Life in a Garrison Town.

Cloth, 6/-; also in Picture Boards, 2/-. (8th Edition.)

"This discursive story, dealing with life in a garrison town, is full of pleasant 'go' and movement which has distinguished 'Bootles' Baby,' 'Pluck,' or in fact a majority of some half-dozen novelettes which the author has submitted to the eyes of railway bookstall patronisers."—*Daily Telegraph.*

"The strength of the book lies in its sketches of life in a garrison town, which are undeniably clever. . . . It is pretty clear that Mr. Winter draws from life."—*St. James's Gazette.*

GARRISON GOSSIP, Gathered in Blankhampton.

(A Sequel to "ARMY SOCIETY.") Cloth, 2/6; also in Picture Boards, 2/-
4th Edition.)

"'Garrison Gossip' may fairly rank with 'Cavalry Life,' and the various other books with which Mr. Winter has so agreeably beguiled our leisure hours."—*Saturday Review.*

"The novel fully maintains the reputation which its author has been fortunate enough to gain in a special line of his own."—*Graphic.*

A SIEGE BABY. Cloth, 2/6; Picture boards, 2/-

"The story which gives its title to this new sheaf of stories by the popular author of 'Bootles' Baby' is a very touching and pathetic one. . . . Amongst the other stories, the one entitled, 'Out of the Mists' is, perhaps, the best written, although the tale of true love it embodies comes to a most melancholy ending."—*County Gentlemen.*

BEAUTIFUL JIM (5th Edition.)

Cloth Gilt, 2/6; also Picture Boards, 2/-.

MRS. BOB. (3rd Edition.)

Cloth gilt, 2/6.

F. V. WHITE & Co., 31, Southampton Street, Strand.

MRS. EDWARD KENNARD'S SPORTING NOVELS.

At all Booksellers and Bookstalls.

MATRON OR MAID. Cloth, 2s. 6d.

LANDING A PRIZE. (3rd Edition.)
Cloth, 2s. 6d.

OUR FRIENDS IN THE HUNTING FIELD.
Cloth, 2/6.

A CRACK COUNTY.
Cloth gilt, 2/6.; also Picture Boards, 2s.

THE GIRL IN THE BROWN HABIT.
Cloth gilt, 2/6; Picture Boards, 2/-. (4th Edition.)

"'Nell Fitzgerald' is an irreproachable heroine, full of gentle womanliness, and rich in all virtues that make her kind estimable. Mrs. Kennard's work is marked by high tone as well as vigorous narrative, and sportsmen, when searching for something new and beguiling for a wet day or spell of frost, can hardly light upon anything better than these fresh and picturesque hunting stories of Mrs. Kennard's."— *Daily Telegraph.*

KILLED IN THE OPEN.
Cloth gilt, 2/6; Picture Boards, 2/-. (3rd Edition.)

"It is in truth a very good love story set in a framework of hounds and horses, but one that could be read with pleasure independently of any such attractions."— *Fortnightly Review.*
"'Killed in the Open' is a very superior sort of hunting novel indeed."—*Graphic.*

STRAIGHT AS A DIE.
Cloth gilt, 2/6; Picture Boards, 2/-. (3rd Edition.)

"If you like sporting novels I can recommend to you Mrs. Kennard's 'Straight as a Die.'"—*Truth.*

A REAL GOOD THING.
Cloth gilt, 2/6. Also Picture Boards, 2/-. (5th Edition.)

"There are some good country scenes and country spins in 'A Real Good Thing.' The hero, poor old Hopkins, is a strong character."—*Academy.*

TWILIGHT TALES. (*Illustrated.*) Cloth gilt, 2/6.

BY THE SAME AUTHOR.
In Paper Cover, 1/-; Cloth, 1/6.

THE MYSTERY OF A WOMAN'S HEART.

A GLORIOUS GALLOP. (Second Edition.)

F. V. WHITE & Co., 31, Southampton Street, Strand.

HAWLEY SMART'S SPORTING NOVELS.
At all Booksellers and Bookstalls.

LONG ODDS.   Cloth gilt, 2/6. (3rd Edition.)

THE MASTER OF RATHKELLY.
Cloth gilt, 2/6. (5th Edition.)

THE OUTSIDER.   Cloth gilt, 2/6. (4th Edition.)

BY THE SAME AUTHOR. Each in Paper Cover, 1/-; Cloth, 1/6.

A BLACK BUSINESS.

THE LAST COUP.   (3rd Edition)

CLEVERLY WON.

NEW NOVELS
By B. L. FARJEON.
In Cloth, 2/6.

A YOUNG GIRL'S LIFE.

TOILERS OF BABYLON.

THE DUCHESS OF ROSEMARY LANE.
By the Author of "Great Porter Square," &c.

In Paper Cover, 1/-; Cloth, 1/6.

THE PERIL OF RICHARD PARDON.

A STRANGE ENCHANTMENT.
By the Author of "Devlin the Barber," &c.

THE HONOURABLE MRS. FETHERSTONHAUCH'S NEW NOVEL.

DREAM FACES.   Cloth, 2/6.
By the Author of "Kilcorran," "Robin Adair," &c.

BRET HARTE'S NEW NOVEL.   Cloth, 2/6; Picture Boards, 2/-.
THE CRUSADE OF THE EXCELSIOR.
By the Author of "The Luck of Roaring Camp," &c.

SIR RANDAL ROBERT'S SPORTING NOVEL.
CURB AND SNAFFLE.   Cloth gilt, 2/6.
By the Author of "In the Shires," &c.

DAUGHTERS OF BELGRAVIA.
By Mrs. ALEXANDER FRASER. Cloth. 2/6.

F. V. WHITE & Co., 31, Southampton Street, Strand.

MRS. ALEXANDER'S NOVELS.

At all Booksellers and Bookstalls.

A FALSE SCENT.

Paper Cover, 1/-; Cloth, 1/6.   (Third Edition.)

A LIFE INTEREST.

Cloth, 2/6. Also Picture Boards, 2/0.

BY WOMAN'S WIT.

(3rd Edition.)   Picture Boards, 2/-.

> "In Mrs. Alexander's tale
> Much art she clearly shows
> In keeping dark the mystery
> Until the story's close!"—*Punch.*

MONA'S CHOICE.   Cloth, 2/6.

"Mrs. Alexander has written a novel quite worthy of her."—*Athenæum.*
". . . . it is pleasant and unaffected."—*Saturday Review.*
"The story is pleasantly told, and some of the subsidiary characters are specially good. Mr. Craig, Mona's uncle, is indeed a triumph of truthful and humorous delineation, and we think that on the whole 'Mona's Choice' must be considered Mrs. Alexander's best novel."—*Spectator.*

"RITA'S" NEW NOVELS.

Each in Paper Cover, 1/-; Cloth, 1/6. At all Booksellers & Bookstalls.

THE DOCTOR'S SECRET.

A VAGABOND LOVER.

THE MYSTERY OF A TURKISH BATH.

(2nd Edition.)

"Every fresh piece of work which 'Rita' publishes, shows an increase of power, and a decided advance on the last. The booklet contains some very smart writing indeed."—*Whitehall Review.*

THE SEVENTH DREAM.   A Romance.

". . . . is a powerful and interesting study in weird effects of fiction. It will hold the close attention of its readers from first to last, and keep them entertained with changing sensations of wonder."—*Scotsman.*

F. V. WHITE & Co., 31, Southampton Street, Strand.

POPULAR WORKS
At all Booksellers' and Bookstalls.

By JOHN STRANGE WINTER.

ARMY SOCIETY.   Life in a Garrison Town.
CLOTH GILT, 6s.

By MRS. ARMSTRONG.
Author of "MODERN ETIQUETTE IN PUBLIC AND PRIVATE," &c.

GOOD FORM. *(2nd Edition).*
A Book of Every Day Etiquette.
LIMP CLOTH, 2s.

By PERCY THORPE.

HISTORY OF JAPAN.
CLOTH, 3s. 6d.

By PARNELL GREENE.

ON THE BANKS OF THE DEE
A Legend of Chester.
CLOTH, 5s.

By W. GERARD.

BYRON RE-STUDIED IN HIS DRAMAS.
CLOTH, 5s.

THE VISION, and Other Poems.
CLOTH, 3s. 6d.

F. V. WHITE & CO., 31, Southampton Street, Strand.

ONE VOLUME NOVELS

BY POPULAR AUTHORS.

Crown 8vo., Cloth 2s. 6d. each.

AT ALL BOOKSELLERS AND BOOKSTALLS.

By JOHN STRANGE WINTER.

MRS. BOB.

BEAUTIFUL JIM.

A SIEGE BABY.

GARRISON GOSSIP.

By MRS. EDWARD KENNARD.

MATRON OR MAID.

LANDING A PRIZE.

A CRACK COUNTY.

OUR FRIENDS IN THE HUNTING-FIELD.

A REAL GOOD THING.

STRAIGHT AS A DIE.

THE GIRL IN THE BROWN HABIT.

KILLED IN THE OPEN.

TWILIGHT TALES.   (*Illustrated.*)

By HAWLEY SMART.

LONG ODDS.

THE MASTER OF RATHKELLY.

THE OUTSIDER.

By B. L. FARJEON.

A YOUNG GIRL'S LIFE.

TOILERS OF BABYLON.

THE DUCHESS OF ROSEMARY LANE

F. V. WHITE & CO., 31, Southampton Street, Strand.

ONE VOLUME NOVELS—*Continued.*

By F. C. PHILIPS & C. J. WILLS.
SYBIL ROSS'S MARRIAGE.

By MRS. ALEXANDER.
A LIFE INTEREST.
MONA'S CHOICE.

By MRS. LOVETT CAMERON.
A LOST WIFE.
THIS WICKED WORLD.
THE COST OF A LIE.
A NORTH COUNTRY MAID.

By JUSTIN M'CARTHY, M.P. & Mrs. CAMPBELL PRAED.
THE LADIES' GALLERY.
THE RIVAL PRINCESS.

By BRET HARTE.
THE CRUSADE OF THE EXCELSIOR.

By the Honble. MRS. FETHERSTONHAUGH.
DREAM FACES.

By FERGUS HUME.
MISS MEPHISTOPHELES.

By Mrs. HUNGERFORD, Author of "MOLLY BAWN."
THE HONBLE. MRS. VEREKER.
A LIFE'S REMORSE.

By "RITA."
SHEBA.

By MRS. ALEXANDER FRASER.
DAUGHTERS OF BELGRAVIA.
SHE CAME BETWEEN.

By MAY CROMMELIN and J. MORAY BROWN.
VIOLET VYVIAN, M.F.H.

F. V. WHITE & CO., 31, Southampton Street, Strand.

" POPULAR " NOVELS.

Picture Boards, 2s. each.

AT ALL BOOKSELLERS AND BOOKSTALLS.

———◆———

BEAUTIFUL JIM. By JOHN STRANGE WINTER,
Author of "Bootles' Baby," &c. (Fifth Edition.)

GARRISON GOSSIP. By the same Author.
(Fourth Edition.)

A SIEGE BABY. By the same Author.
(Fourth Edition.)

ARMY SOCIETY ; Or, Life in a Garrison Town.
By the same Author. (Eighth Edition.)

THE MASTER OF RATHKELLY. By HAWLEY
SMART. (Fifth Edition.)

A LIFE INTEREST. By Mrs. ALEXANDER,
Author of "The Wooing O't," &c. (Third
Edition.)

THE GIRL IN THE BROWN HABIT. By
Mrs. EDWARD KENNARD, Author of "A Real Good
Thing," "A Crack County," &c. (Fifth Edition.)

F. V. WHITE & Co., 31, Southampton Street, Strand.

"POPULAR" NOVELS—*(continued).*

A REAL GOOD THING. By the same
Author. (Sixth Edition.)

KILLED IN THE OPEN. By the same
Author. (Sixth Edition.)

STRAIGHT AS A DIE. By the same Author.
(Sixth Edition.)

A CRACK COUNTY. By the same Author.
(Fifth Edition.)

IN A GRASS COUNTRY: A Story of Love
and Sport. By Mrs. H. LOVETT CAMERON.
(Eighth Edition.)

A DEVOUT LOVER. By the same Author.
(Second Edition.)

THE COST OF A LIE. By the same Author.
(Second Edition.)

A DEAD PAST. By the same Author.

THE CRUSADE OF THE "EXCELSIOR."
By BRET HARTE, Author of "Devil's Ford," &c.

THE HONBLE. MRS. VEREKER. By the
Author of "Molly Bawn," "A Life's Remorse," &c.

MISS MEPHISTOPHELES. By FERGUS HUME,
Author of "The Mystery of a Hansom Cab,"
"Madame Midas," &c.

A WOMAN'S FACE. By FLORENCE WARDEN,
Author of "The House on the Marsh," &c.

ONE SHILLING NOVELS.

In Paper Cover. Cloth, 1s. 6d.
At all Booksellers' and Bookstalls.

FERRERS COURT. By JOHN STRANGE WINTER, Author of "Bootles' Baby."

BUTTONS. By the same Author. (Fifth Edition.)

A LITTLE FOOL. By the same Author. (Seventh Edition.)

THE PICCADILLY PUZZLE. By FERGUS HUME, Author of "The Mystery of a Hansom Cab," &c.

MY WONDERFUL WIFE! A STUDY IN SMOKE. By MARIE CORELLI, Author of "A Romance of Two Worlds," &c. (Second Edition.)

A TROUBLESOME GIRL. By Mrs. HUNGERFORD, Author of "Molly Bawn," &c. (Fifth Edition.)

HER LAST THROW. By the same Author.

A STRANGE ENCHANTMENT. By. B. L. FARJEON, Author of "Devlin the Barber," &c.

THE PERIL OF RICHARD PARDON. By the same Author.

A FRENCH MARRIAGE By F. C. PHILIPS, Author of "As in a Looking Glass," &c.

A VAGABOND LOVER. By "RITA," Author of "The Mystery of a Turkish Bath," &c.

THE LAST COUP. (Third Edition.) By HAWLEY SMART, Author of "Cleverly Won," &c.

A BLACK BUSINESS. By the same Author.

A FALSE SCENT. (Third Edition.) By Mrs. ALEXANDER.

ONE SHILLING NOVELS—*(continued)*.

MY POOR DICK. (Fifth Edition.) By JOHN STRANGE WINTER. (With Illustrations by MAURICE GREIFFENHAGEN.)

BOOTLES' CHILDREN. (Seventh Edition.) By JOHN STRANGE WINTER. (With Illustrations by J. BERNARD PARTRIDGE.)

THE CONFESSIONS OF A PUBLISHER. By the same Author.

MIGNON'S HUSBAND. (Tenth Edition.) By the same Author.

THAT IMP. (Eighth Edition.) By the same Author.

MIGNON'S SECRET. (Thirteenth Edition.) By the same Author.

ON MARCH. (Seventh Edition.) By the same Author.

IN QUARTERS. (Eighth Edition.) By the same Author.

A GLORIOUS GALLOP. (Second Edition.) By Mrs. EDWARD KENNARD.

THE MYSTERY OF A WOMAN'S HEART. By the same Author.

THE MYSTERY OF A TURKISH BATH. (Second Edition.) By "Rita."

THE DOCTOR'S SECRET. By the same Author.

THE SEVENTH DREAM. A Romance. By the same Author.

DEVIL'S FORD. By BRET HARTE.

TOM'S WIFE. By Lady MARGARET MAJENDIE, Author of "Fascination," &c.

IN A GRASS COUNTRY. By Mrs. H. LOVETT CAMERON. (Ninth Edition.)

THE CONFESSIONS OF A DOOR MAT. By ALFRED C. CALMOUR, Author of "The Amber Heart," &c.

www.ingramcontent.com/pod-product-compliance
Lightning Source LLC
Chambersburg PA
CBHW030121030726
47498CB00007B/2491